STRAIGHT
FROM THE
HEART

Letters of Hope and Inspiration from Survivors of Breast Cancer

STRAIGHT
FROM THE
HEART

Ina Yalof

KENSINGTON BOOKS

KENSINGTON BOOKS are published by

Kensington Publishing Corp.
850 Third Avenue
New York, NY 10022

Library of Congress Card Catalog Number: 96-076487
ISBN 1-57566-094-6

First Printing: October, 1996
10 9 8 7 6 5 4 3 2 1

Printed in the United States of America

For Esther, Jean and Peggy—whose spirit and courage continue to inspire me

and for Leslie

"*When you get into a tight place and everything goes against you, 'til it seems as though you could not hold on a moment longer, never give up then, for that is just the place and time that the tide will turn.*"
—Harriet Beecher Stowe

"*I believe that in years to come, when breast cancer is behind us, we, whose number came up and who were too late for prevention or cure, will all be mentioned briefly in some medical journal or history book in no very significant way. So, I am glad to speak now . . .*"
—Dorothy Nihart

INTRODUCTION

The ability to talk openly about breast cancer is a recent phenomenon. For years, women hid their physical scars behind padded bras and kept their emotional wounds to themselves. If they knew no one close to them who had experienced this disease, they toughed it out alone. Many were not so tough.

Today breast cancer has taken center stage. Much of the credit for throwing back the curtain must go to Betty Ford and Happy Rockefeller. These two women, both very much in the public eye, openly acknowledged that this is a disease like any other. Their willingness to discuss it publicly was followed by other high-profile women such as Nancy Reagan, Erma Bombeck, Shirley Temple Black, Gloria Steinem, Linda Ellerbe, and Olivia Newton-John. And the list goes on.

While the last generation saw the stigma of having breast cancer erased, this generation's breast cancer survivors, their families and friends, are demanding funds to fight the disease and find its cure. Today, activist groups can be found storming Capitol Hill, where the competition for scarce medical-research dollars takes place, or clustered on village greens across the United States, where local politicians must hear their voices. In the early seventies, when Betty Ford and Happy Rockefeller went public about their breast cancer, one of every thirteen women was destined to develop the disease over the period of her lifetime. Since that time, despite billions of dollars spent in cancer research, the breast cancer incidence in this country has grown by 2 percent per year. Today, unfortunately, the rallying cry of the breast cancer activist is "One in Nine."

Few are left untouched by this disease. If it hasn't happened to us, or to our mother or to our sister or to our daughter, it most certainly has happened to someone else we care—or cared—about. Breast cancer clearly plays no favorites. It transcends the American spectrum, tapping black women and white, educated and uneducated, rich and poor, single, married, and divorced. It affects those at high risk and those with no risk factors at all.

What happens when breast cancer strikes? In her letter, T. J. England writes about hearing her diagnosis: "I entered the terrifying new world of oncology medicine. In this new world, estrogen receptors, tumor markers, CAT scans, blood counts and other tests became the markers that determined what the course of my disease and my days would hold."

No one is prepared to hear the words "you have breast cancer." Decisions need to be made almost immediately, treatments decided upon, a new language learned. With that single sentence, a woman is immediately transformed from "vibrant human being" into "cancer patient." The emotional effects can be devastating.

Treatment is attended by other issues. Surgery alters a

woman's body image and robs her of her self-esteem. Radiation schedules must be adhered to. Chemotherapy takes its toll. Then, usually six to eight months later, treatment ends. Oddly enough, this sparks a whole *new* set of concerns. Women who have felt secure in their ties to their physicians and their rigid schedule of treatments are suddenly cut loose. No longer active in the fight against their disease, they find themselves in a quandary: Now what? What if it comes back? How will I know? It is now, perhaps more than during treatment, that women need emotional reinforcement and comfort.

I am a medical sociologist as well as a writer. In the fifteen years that I have worked with breast cancer patients and their surgeons, one of the most important things I have learned is this: Women who have breast cancer can be surrounded by the best doctors in the world and can have the most supportive family and friends, but what they really want is company of their own kind. They want to know that others have gotten through this; that it may be normal, for example, to rail out at your husband at the times when you love him the most; that most single women wonder about the "right time" to tell a date about her mastectomy; that everyone fears for her future and that that apprehension rarely goes away.

This book provides the opportunity for those of you who have had breast cancer—and for those of you who are close to someone coping with the disease—to read firsthand accounts of others who have faced the same problems, known the same struggles, and had the same doubts and fears.

The letters included here take us into the world of the newly diagnosed woman, where the threat of death is closely linked to the loss of control. The writers vacillate between their fear of recurrence and their renewed appreciation for life. We learn how the loss of a breast leads them to search for who they are and to ultimately discover what is really meaningful in their lives.

This book began with the reading of a magazine article in early 1993. At the time I was working on another book about breast cancer—more of a consumer's guide—with Dr. Irene Kuter, an oncologist at the Massachusetts General Hospital in Boston. While researching the book, I happened to read *McCall's* magazine's October 1993 issue. Because October is National Breast Cancer Awareness Month, the magazine had four excellent articles specific to the subject. In her "Letter from the Editor," Kate White wrote: "If you are a breast cancer survivor, we would love to hear from you."

I had a feeling that single sentence would bring a windfall of responses. First, because women are no longer hesitant to talk about their personal experiences, and secondly, because I believed that survivors of anything—and most certainly breast cancer—would want to shout about it from the rooftops. Wouldn't it be great, I thought, if I could use short quotes from some of those letters to sprinkle throughout the book I was writing. They would lend precisely the human touch I felt was missing in what promised to be a somewhat technical guide to the disease, its diagnosis and treatment. I closed the magazine, picked up the telephone, and called one of the editors at *McCall's*. I described my project and asked if she would allow me to read some of the letters.

Three days later a large brown package arrived in my mailbox. I remember standing at the kitchen table, still in my winter coat, pulling open the wrapping and spilling over three hundred envelopes onto the table. The envelopes were thick and thin, large and small, plain and fancy. They were pink, white, blue, and brown. Return addresses were scrawled in pencil, typed on old-fashioned typewriters, or printed with the fanciest of laser printers. Some came from Dallas and Brooklyn and Chicago and L.A., but many had postmarks from places I had never heard of—Gastonia, North Carolina; Loves Park, Illinois; Arvada, Colorado; Vandling, Pennsylvania.

The seeds from which this book grew were sown with the first letter I opened. It was a short letter—less than two pages. The writer was thirty-four. "At first," she wrote, "I thought my life would end. Cancer sounds so final. My son was only four years old. I had no intention of leaving him behind. I must fight this cancer." And fight it she did, with all that science had to offer her. Chemotherapy for six months, radiation for two. When it was over, her hair just long enough to comb with a washcloth, she took a trip, regained the seventeen pounds she had lost, and went back to work as a detective in the New York City Police Department. Sleeping became easier, she said, as cancer was not on her mind all the time. "Yesterday I received a call from my doctor advising me that according to all the tests there are no traces of cancer. There are so many things to do and plans to make." And she ended her letter with six words that stay with me to this day, words that I believe sum up the theme of this book: "Life goes on for Esther Del Vecchio."

The next letter I read was from Helen Hansen, who had had a radical mastectomy in 1968. The day before surgery she planted a hedge of fifty rosebushes along her fence. "They are still there," she wrote, "and I am still here—after twenty-five years." Jean Maynard's ten-page, single-spaced discourse was overflowing with personal anecdotes, coping tips, and inspirational messages. And there was humor throughout, even as she addressed her child's feelings. "I thank God for my son, a fifteen-year old who managed to continue to treat me as all teenagers do their mothers at this stage of life. It helps keep you grounded in reality. I know that he had fears, and I know that I was prayed for and loved by him even though he wasn't always able to tell me. Unfortunately for him, it looks like I'll be around for a long time to continue to be the bane of his existence!"

As I continued to read, something significant struck me. There were letters here from women who had had their cancer as long ago as fifty-five years! Why, I wondered, would anyone want to resurrect an event of so long ago? And how could she recall it so vividly? But I soon saw that one never forgets. Even the date of the day a woman hears she has cancer is forever burned into her memory. "It's like the day of your wedding or the birth of your child," wrote one woman. "It never leaves you."

There was something else. The length, depth, and personal nature of these letters just didn't seem to be consistent with what one would write to something so impersonal as a national magazine. Yet there they were. Hundreds of them. And even the shortest spoke volumes. They described the value of family and friends and the rewards of sharing with other women who have had breast cancer. There were tales of husbands who left and husbands whose unending devotion was beyond words. Many, many women described life on this side of breast cancer as being different—frightening, tenuous, exhausting—but mostly joyous in the discovery that every day brings its own gifts.

Some letters were written in the heat of battle, others in the repose of retrospect. Ten percent contained enclosures. There were letters to friends, essays, articles by and about them. Quite a few women sent pictures of themselves. Linda Jordan wore a bikini to show off her new reconstruction. Janet Meyer, who is still tap dancing at age sixty five, was dressed in a pink and blue satin majorette costume. Kim Cassidy, who had only one child before breast cancer and chemotherapy, sent a picture of herself buried under her four small children on the couch in her living room. "This," she wrote, "is what my life is all about."

After reading twenty or so of the letters, I stacked them in piles on the table beside my desk and returned to my project at hand.

Nineteen ninety-three was the snowiest winter on record in Boston. As the weeks went on, I continued to work on the Massachusetts General Hospital book. Topics from "Understanding the role of DNA in a cancer cell" to "Chemotherapy's side effects" filled my computer. The quotes I was planning to take from the letters would be decided upon when the book was finished.

The snow kept falling. There were days when I didn't get out. Every so often, if I put in a particularly long stint at my desk, I would pull a few of the letters from the pile as a reward, open them, and savor their contents. The more I read, the more I wondered: How, from so many, could I possibly select only the fifteen or twenty quotes I needed? How could I distill a letter down to just a quote or two. How could I leave such priceless material behind?

I soon became certain of two things. These letters were not

put in my path by accident. And I was going to put them in a book—their own book.

Once I had decided to compile a book of letters it became important to get a well-rounded sampling of correspondence from women other than those who read *McCall's*. In an effort to solicit letters on my own, I wrote to the editors of newsletters from national cancer organizations such as Y-Me and the National Breast Cancer Coalition. I also wrote to the excellent magazine for all cancer survivors, *Coping*. In time, a whole new batch of letters arrived. I was astonished by how closely they resembled the letters I already had. More enclosures, more letters to friends, more coping tips.

With some difficulty, I selected ninety-two letters from the combined group. I wrote each woman and enclosed release forms for permission to use her words to be signed and returned to me. This I did with some minor trepidation. After all, it was now a year since many of the women had written their original letters. Would they remember?

The signed releases began arriving almost immediately. Four the first day, ten the next. And with them, more often than not, came new letters. Long ones, too. There were updates on themselves and their families. One woman had won her lawsuit against her radiologist for two misdiagnoses. "I'm free, now, to speak of it," she said. And she did. Several had new babies. A few had had recurrences. And far more than fifty percent expressed gratitude for the opportunity to touch others.

By the end of the fourth week, eighty-three women had replied. I scrambled for phone numbers and tried calling the remaining nine. Eventually I reached eight of them. "Just didn't get around to it yet," Patty Andrew said. "Oh, no problem," was my answer. "No rush at all." What I meant, of course, was this: Thank God you're okay and illness is not the reason you didn't reply.

By the end of two months, all but ninety-eight-year-old Mary Brittain were accounted for. I had my doubts about finding her but decided to try to track her down anyway. The long-distance operator said there was no longer a phone listing at the address she had given. But because my original letter to her did not come back, I decided to write her again. This time I enclosed a stamped self-addressed envelope, plus directions on the front to please forward if possible. And lo and behold, what should arrive the following week? A signed release from the lady from La Grange Park, Illinois. So that's it. All ninety-two accounted for. One year later. One hundred percent. Simply amazing.

I narrowed the number of letters down to seventy-two, mostly because of space constraints. This proved to be one of the hardest parts of writing this book. Leaving even one word behind made me feel as though I was discarding a precious gem.

You will notice that some of the letters carry first names and towns and some carry full names. I offered a choice to the women as to how they wanted their letters signed. You will notice, too, that there is no table of contents. Because most letters address a multiple of subjects and overlap more often than not, I chose to include a cross-referenced index instead. This allows you to turn immediately to a letter containing information on a specific subject if that is what you are seeking.

I got to know many of the women over the telephone, and met Esther Del Vecchio and her husband over breakfast one morning in Brooklyn. She was recovering from a second go-round of chemotherapy and was facing a bone marrow transplant in the near future. She wore a cap over a quarter-inch growth of hair, but even without it she is a very beautiful woman with a dazzling smile and a great attitude. "What have you learned from all of us?" she wanted to know. What were the common threads that ran through these letters? I told her there were so many things, far too many to enumerate, but I could come up with two themes that were on my mind a lot. The first was contained in her simple phrase that continues to touch me in its applicability to so many breast cancer survivors: "Life goes on for Esther Del Vecchio." The second was of the greatest importance for every woman to hear and believe: "A diagnosis of breast cancer is not a death sentence." These words were written directly by both Nancy Arnold and Cathy Jo Gove and implied by so many others. And here, I thought, are 72 women—some of whom heard otherwise many years ago—who are living proof of those words.

When you write a book you are implying two things. First, that you have something to say, and second, that you are the one to say it. I turn over the baton to the women herein on both counts. I am not the writer. I simply acted as editor and provided the stage. They are the ones who have made the music

Ina Yalof
Boston, Massachusetts

I had my left breast removed in October 1938—fifty-five years ago.

I was pregnant with my third child and the tumor had grown with my pregnancy. After the baby was born, I had a mastectomy. The surgeon told my family I had about two months to live. He had my husband come to the hospital to have Thanksgiving dinner with me—thinking it was my last. He then decided to radiate my ovaries, hoping it might help. I was in the hospital over a month.

I was sterile for ten years when I discovered I was pregnant again. I had a healthy baby girl on March 19, 1949.

My children are now 60, 57, 55, and 44 years old.

Sincerely,
Mrs. Alice "Carey" Tucker
Quincy, Massachusetts

I truly welcome this chance to stand up and be counted with the Breast Cancer Survivors. I believe that in years to come, when breast cancer is all behind us, we, whose number came up and who were too late for prevention or the cure, will all be mentioned briefly and jointly in some medical journal or medical history book in no very significant way. So, I am glad to speak now. . . .

I'm sixty-eight years old. I had my first mastectomy on Christmas Eve 1985. (Christmas Eve because the operating rooms were available that day, and I chose not to wait.) My second mastectomy was performed July 15, 1993, seven and a half years later. I was very disappointed this time because I thought I was through with cancer. I wanted to be like my mother who lived twenty-eight years after a radical mastectomy when she was sixty and died of a heart ailment at the age of eighty-eight.

Of course, "Why me, Lord?" came to my mind. But I got the response, "Why not you? You've had it so good for so long. Why should the bad things always happen to someone else?"

As I convalesced, events kept happening that I knew would be so much harder than breast cancer to bear— A schoolteacher I had greatly admired went on trial for a sex crime committed fourteen years earlier. "That's worse," I thought. Terrorists shot up an Italian airport, killing women and children in a senseless massacre. "That is definitely worse," I concluded. A child was kidnapped, and I thanked God I wasn't its mother.

I felt I was expected to be devastated, but something inside me refused to cooperate. Perhaps it was my will to live or just realizing that I had to accept the inevitable that kept me from railing out against what happened to me. Maybe it was something as simple as knowing my mother got through it.

After my first mastectomy I focused primarily on getting back to my classroom and my normal life. I was amazed at how quickly I accommodated to the physical changes. This time, though, I have had to come to terms with my mortality. It has made me realize how precious every day is. I love life more now than I ever took time to love it before. I walk, I enjoy the sounds, the sights, the smells; and I sometimes wonder what lies ahead. It's like the old song that keeps coming back to me: *Que será, será . . . What ever will be, will be.*

Dorothy Nihart
Auburn, California

Like so many other breast cancer survivors, I am writing this letter in hopes that it may find its way into someone's hands who is going through an experience similar to mine and can benefit from my story.

I discovered a lump myself in the spring of 1989, less than a year after I was married and while my husband and I were trying to start a family. Like so many women in my age group (I was thirty-seven at the time), I had postponed having a family until I had obtained a high-powered career position in a Fortune 500 company in Southern California. So now I was reaching the time that I really needed to get things moving. I was in that low-risk group, nothing in my family. I had grown up eating the healthiest of home-cooked meals in Alaska and had barely seen a doctor except for my annual checkups.

To make a long story short, the lump turned out to be malignant, and within a month I had undergone a mastectomy (with reconstruction) and started six "long" months of chemotherapy. Throughout the whole ordeal, I kept asking my doctors if I could still have a baby, and they pretty much refused to give me a clear or direct answer. The only thing that they warned me of was that the chemotherapy often sent your body into premature menopause, which would then make it impossible. I also found it difficult to find oth-

4

ers who had been through this and had subsequently had children, leading me to believe that it probably wouldn't happen. Everyone tried to be nice by saying, "You can always adopt," but the reality of obtaining a baby through adoption when you are over forty and have had breast cancer, is not highly probable. And I knew that.

At the sixth month of chemotherapy, I did go into menopause, which was confirmed several months afterwards. So my husband and I began dealing with the reality that we would not be able to have the children we had hoped for.

Several months later, though, my periods reappeared. No one knows why or how. The doctors still didn't give me much hope and again cautioned me about getting pregnant. There were factors revolving around the hormone fluctuations that take place during pregnancy, and it was unclear how they may relate to breast cancer.

Well, I am now forty-two and have a beautiful two-year old son, and he will be having a brother two months from now. I feel wonderful, and my checkups have been normal. I have also quit my high-paying, high-stress job, and, although I still enjoy working outside the home, I am concentrating on raising my family and enjoying this new chapter in my life.

Yours truly,
Jette Schuh
Albuquerque, New Mexico

I found the lumps in my breasts two years ago—one day after my father's death. There is a history of breast cancer in my family. My favorite aunt died of the illness just a few years ago. I have advanced fibrocystic disease and have done a self-examination every month for years. For some time, I'd felt that I was a time bomb just waiting to explode. Still, I was stunned when the radiologist told me that I had a malignant tumor.

At first my diagnosis was grave. The biopsy revealed that the tumor, slightly smaller than two centimeters, was no longer encapsulated within the tumor walls and had begun to invade the surrounding tissue and probably the lymph nodes. I was scheduled for surgery on December 27, the day that would have been my father's sixty-fifth birthday.

In the interim between diagnosis and surgery, I thought about a lot of things. I thought about dying—but mostly I thought about living. I thought about my daughter. She was fifteen at the time, and I felt she still needed me. I worried about the cost of the surgery. Would I need a leave of absence from my job? Would I live long enough to take that leave of absence? Would I get to be a part of my granddaughter's life? I prayed, believe me, I prayed that I would live and I asked God to give me the strength I needed to survive.

I had my surgery and went home early. One week later, my husband and I watched anxiously as the pathologist's report regarding my tumor rolled off the fax machine in my doctor's office. My doctor and every member of his staff stood there with me. There wasn't a sound in the office other than the hum of the machine. All of us there, waiting breathlessly. I will never forget my doctor's reading that report aloud, naming the parts of my breast and responding with, "No cancer; no signs of cancer." He paused when he got to the results about the lymph nodes. My heart skipped a beat. He looked at me, eyes moist with tears, and replied, "No cancer." It was the first time I cried through the whole ordeal. I will never forget those words.

My doctors and I decided that I would follow up with adjuvant chemotherapy. I had nine treatments. Chemo was tougher than surgery. I was ill but very glad to be alive. I did not lose my hair. Toward the end of the treatments, it was becoming increasingly difficult to fight illnesses—due to the low white blood cell count. Drugs used in chemotherapy destroy the good guys as well as the bad and, despite the use of a new antinausea drug called Zophran, I was so sick at my stomach. It was a nausea I've never experienced before or since—intense, wrenching, and relentless. How I managed to gain twenty-six pounds instead of lose weight remains somewhat of a mystery to me.

These days I pursue life aggressively. I no longer put off until tomorrow what I want, need, or desire to do today. I intend to live.

My husband and I spend more time together. We talk now—really talk. We take walks in the moonlight, and we wander up and down the beach along the shores of Lake Erie. We watch the sun set. It doesn't take very long, you know—the sun sets quickly—like the hours in our lives.

The love my daughter and I have for each other has grown. Of course, we still have our moments when we disagree, but we also take whatever time we need to work through those disagreements because we both know the time we have together is precious. Sometimes we stay up all night, just talking. I guess you could call it our own private little slumber parties. We go out to lunch together once a week—just the two of us.

One of my most memorable moments during recovery

came when she showed me a paper she had written in English. It was an essay about heroes. She wrote that I was her hero. She said she thought I had courage and that I inspired her. Her words touched me deeply . . . because any courage I might have demonstrated came from the strength and love and support that was given to me by her, her dad, my son, and my friends.

And my son, the soldier, never ends a phone call without telling me he loves me. When we see each other I get the most genuine, heartfelt hugs. It used to make him feel uncomfortable to do that. It doesn't anymore.

I recall the first time I was ill after my chemotherapy treatments had ceased. Fearing a recurrence, my daughter called my son, who called my doctor, who called me. That's when I realized that cancer is a family thing. Cancer (and the fear of cancer) also touches the lives of the people who love and care about me. It is as important for families to communicate their feelings and fears and anger over this life-threatening illness as it is to share their love and affection with the victim.

Jim, my husband, is an amateur photographer. Frequently, he carries a camera with him. Before cancer, I always hated having my picture taken. The odds of getting a smile out of me were about as good as my winning the lottery. Today, when my husband asks me to pose for a picture, you'd better believe I grin. My daughter and I often pose together. I know now that those photos will be memories—memories of beautiful moments we've shared together. I plan to keep on smiling. I anticipate that I'll be around when I'm eighty-five. I'm going to dance at my grand-daughter's wedding.

Yours,
Peggy Boozer
Lake City, Pennsylvania

I was one month shy of my thirty-fourth birthday when I was diagnosed with breast cancer. It came as a surprise to all of us as I only had one risk factor: early onset of menstruation. There was no family history.

I spent the next three weeks undergoing a battery of tests to ensure there was no spread of the disease. There wasn't. The mass that was removed during the biopsy was almost two centimeters. Three of the four sides showed no cancerous cells in the outer edge, but one side showed cancer all the way to the edge. That made me a borderline case. They gave me the choice of a modified radical mastectomy or a lumpectomy.

I was thirty-three, divorced, and had no permanent relationship—no man in my life to tell me he'd love me anyway and that I'd never be alone. What I thought I faced was the possibility that no man would ever love me again. I knew that the choice of lumpectomy was clearly one of vanity for me. But the safest, most aggressive action was the mastectomy. Finally, I came to the realization that it wouldn't matter if a man did or did not love me if I wasn't alive to enjoy it. I chose the mastectomy, and a feeling of peace and security came over me. And I never looked back or doubted my choice. I wanted to know that, if some time down the road I have a recurrence, I could be certain that

I had done everything possible. I had six months of chemotherapy, working full-time throughout. I gained thirty-five pounds, lost half my hair, and suffered hot flashes from menopause induced by the chemo.

But I did it! I've had reconstructive surgery, lost the weight, and regained my full head of hair. I look and feel better now than at any other time in my adult life. I have a confidence in myself now that I never had before. I realize that I can face anything, with strength and dignity.

I've also been pleasantly surprised by the male species. They simply don't seem to care that I'm different. They never reacted negatively either before or after the reconstructive surgery. They continued to support and pursue. My male friends got me through this with my self-image intact. They were wonderful.

Breast cancer is a twofold attack. It threatens your life but it also threatens your concept of femininity, sexuality, and who you are. But when you come out on the other side, you have a better understanding and a deeper appreciation for both. No major life changes—just an inner peace that wasn't there before. You make sure that your loved ones know they're loved, and you stop procrastinating. Life is good, and you learn to appreciate each day.

Yours sincerely,
Dawn Chastain
Folsom, California

*W*oman is *not* the weaker sex!

To learn she has cancer . . .
To undergo this surgery . . .
The bone scans, marrow tests, radiation, chemo . . .
And then to hold her breath that it won't recur . . .

I had a radical mastectomy almost twenty-five years ago. It was a time when no one wanted to talk about breast cancer. But *I* did. So I became a Reach to Recovery volunteer. The experience has enabled me to come in contact with the most beautiful women, each of whom has her own story. Many of us are still in touch with one another. On different occasions, "anniversaries," or a recurrence—happy or sad—we share our common bond. I also volunteer two days a week at a local hospital, in Oncology. It's my payment for living on this fantastic earth.

> Straight from the heart,
> Viola E.
> Kenilworth, New Jersey

Ruby Ewald is a writer from Sylvania, Ohio. This journal is an account of her breast cancer experience.

Saturday morning, September 7

I lean over the ironing board, brush my right breast in the process, and find the lump. My mind curdles.

Don't panic.

Do a breast examination before you jump to conclusions.

Just because your mother died of ovarian cancer doesn't mean *you* will.

The lump doesn't move or roll when I press it. What could that mean?

Bob and I are enjoying retirement. Now, maybe, I will be looking at death face-to-face.

How can I just up and die?

Saturday afternoon, September 7

I tell Bob about the lump. He knows I'm worried. He thinks it might be another fibrosis problem. Offers to go with me to the internist's office. I turn down the offer.

Monday morning, September 9

I call internist. It's a holiday.

Tuesday morning, September 10

Call internist again. I go directly to his office. He calls a surgeon. Appointment made for September 16th. Three days have elapsed since I discovered the lump. Pressure building. Got to keep busy. I expect the worst.

Thursday, September 12

Energy level too high. Nerves jangled. Bob keeps me busy with golf.

Sunday, September 15

My mind is racing: There's a lump in your right breast.
You have an appointment with a good surgeon.
You have overcome a lot of obstacles.
You have cancer in the family. It's your turn now.
Run, don't walk. Get the heck out of here.
You don't have to see anybody.
What do you know about this doctor stranger?

Monday, September 16

I'm at the surgeon's office. I'm a wreck. He inserts a needle in the lump, draws out tissue. He'll call me when he receives the results of the test. His eyes say there's a problem.

Tuesday, September 17

Bob and I stay close. We're both lost in worry.

Wednesday, September 18

I answer the phone. It's the surgeon. No more waiting. Feel relieved. I choke out the words to my husband, "I have cancer." Bob cradles me in his arms.

I must tell my children. Not tomorrow, but now. I agonize over the phone calls. I call Marcie first. She asks, "Did I cause you to have cancer?" My reply is a retort. "Well, if you have the answer to why people have cancer, you're smarter than all the doctors in the medical field. No, you didn't have anything to do with it; it just came all by itself."

The next call was to our second daughter, Connie. I explained that I had cancer. There was a pause. Connie said, "I want to go with you and Dad when you have the tests." I ask, "Are you sure you want to spend all day at the hospital?" She replies, "Sure. Dad will need me to be with him."

Joyce, our youngest daughter, will graduate from nurses' training in October. I brief her about the test results.

I can't call our son, Steve. I don't know why. I call Joyce again. She does the dirty work for me.

Monday morning, September 23

I enter the hospital. Bob and Connie are with me. I am having a bone scan, cardiac test, bilateral mammography, and chest X rays. A shot of dye is given to me. Two hours and thirty minutes later the bone scan begins. It doesn't hurt. I am on a table, fully clothed. Machine will show if the cancer has spread to any other part of my body.

Monday afternoon, September 23

The X-ray technicians hang up the pictures of mammogram. I remark, "See that white spot? That's the vulture . . . cancer."

Tuesday, October 8

Bob and I are in the surgical waiting area. The surgeon explains the procedures. I am mesmerized by his words, "After the lump is tested I will know how to proceed."

Will I buckle under the strain? How will I feel if I look down and find a part of me missing? Will my husband still love me? I dare not express my fears to anyone. Other family members are living their own private hell. No time to get blubbery.

I wake up in the recovery room. I mumble, "Am I all together?" The answer is yes.

Wednesday, October 9

It's over. I sleep more than I'm awake. Pain shots come

17

regularly. Bob is with me. Nurse tells me a tube is inserted in my side. It drains into a grenade-shaped container. She shows me how to dump the grenade. I tell her she needs to wear gloves. She replies, "I don't use them unless I have to."

Thursday, October 10

The team of doctors comes into my room. I can go home.

Friday, October 11

My first day home. It's wonderful.

Sunday, October 13

I spike a temp. Doctor is called.

Monday, October 14

I've been put on a high-powered antibiotic.

Wednesday, October 16

Back to the doctor's office. He suspects a staph infection. I must return to the hospital.

Thursday, October 17

I'm so sore. Everything is a blur. I can't believe I'm in the hospital again.

Friday, October 18

Thoughts are broken. Losing track of time. I'm being transported to surgery. Breast needs to be lanced.

Saturday, October 19

I feel terrible.

Sunday, October 20

It is confirmed. I have a staph infection. My incision is parting and infection is oozing out. Bob and I cling to each other.

Monday, October 21

The surgeon is in my room, along with a student. Another lancing needs to be done, this time in my bed. A shot of Novocain and the cutting begins. The fluid pours out. I awake three hours later and feel as if the Rock of Gibraltar has been removed from my chest.

Tuesday, October 22

I have some unprofessional blood-pullers. Kick one of them out of my room. She chose a large needle for my small vein. Head nurse appears and asks what's wrong. I tell her I will rip off my bandage and leave this place if one more incompetent technician touches me. She remarks, "You must be joking." I inform her this is no joke. She can watch me walk down the hall.

Wednesday, October 23

I have a temporary full-time needle in my arm. IVs are given frequently.

Thursday, October 24

Seem to be improving.

Friday, October 26

I can go home today! I check out of the hospital.

Thursday, November 7

The head of the radiation department makes a statement. He informs me that there is a chance I'll crack a rib if I sneeze. I wonder why I'm consenting to proceed.

Tuesday, November 12

I start to get cold feet. Tomorrow radiation treatments begin. Doubt runs through my mind. Did I choose the correct road to recovery? Susie, my mentor, has had cancer twice. She says, "Don't let them burn you." These words are carved into my head.

Wednesday, November 13

First radiation treatment. Oncology nurse looks for signs of depression. Will not let her pick my brain. I will remain positive.

Monday, December 16

I'm in the oncology waiting room. I demand to see the doctor before going into the radiation room. Because my breast looks as if it might blister, the doctor orders one week of resting the skin.

Monday, December 23

The oncology doctor is examining me. I ask, "Why are my breast and arm so swollen?" He answers, "It must be from the operation."

Monday, December 30

Checkup is due today with the surgeon. I ask, "Why are my breast and arm so swollen?" He replies, "It could be from the radiation treatments."

Tuesday, December 31

I'm thinking about stopping radiation treatments but decide to continue.

Thursday, January 9

Today is the last treatment!

Sunday, January 12

Bob and I fly to Florida.

Monday, January 27

Breast is swollen and inflamed. Pain is excruciating. I will not give up. I will fight back.

Tuesday, January 28

The Florida doctor won't treat me without my medical records. I call the hospital back home and the oncology nurse answers. Ask her to fax my records. She replies, "Faxing your records would not be financially feasible." I explode, "I'm talking pain, honey! Fax those records and do it today."

Wednesday, January 29

The doctor in Florida tells me I have cellulitis, and a bruised breast. I ask, "How did my breast get bruised?" He answers, "A bruised breast is another term for burned breast. Take these pain pills and antibiotics. You will heal."

Thursday, October 8

I'm at the surgeon's office for another checkup. It's one year since the lumpectomy. After the examination I hurry to the car to share the good news with Bob. I am CAN-CER FREE.

Ruby Ewald

Esther Del Vecchio is a New York City policewoman. She, her husband Frank, and her eight-year-old son Frankie live in Brooklyn.

I was diagnosed with breast cancer on October 6, 1992. At first I thought my life would end. Cancer sounds so final. My son was only four years old! I had no intention of leaving him behind. I must fight this cancer.

I received a lumpectomy on my left breast (one positive lymph node out of fourteen). I was on a six-month chemotherapy program, which required a three-day stay each month at the hospital. I was very ill from the chemotherapy. I lost a lot of weight and all my hair fell out. I looked and felt terrible. But never once was I alone. I had the best support group anyone could ask for—my husband, family, friends, and my four-year old son. He was my biggest inspiration for getting better.

When chemotherapy ended I received radiation for two months. Finally, on July 6, 1993, it was over. Seven days later I celebrated my thirty-ninth birthday with a party and a trip to Cancún with three of my best girlfriends. It was wonderful. Then, my husband, son, and I went to Disneyland. In time, I gained the weight back that I lost (seventeen pounds) and went back to work as a detective with the New York City Police Department. Sleeping became a lot easier, and cancer was not on my mind all the time. And I now have hair to comb.

I now feel that I can do almost anything if I set my mind to it. I love life, and I want to hold on to it as long as I can. I'm a better person to myself and to those around me. Some of my priorities have changed for the better. I am making all kinds of plans with my life because I know I will see them through.

Yesterday, I received a call from my doctor, advising me that, according to all the tests I have taken, there are no traces of cancer. There are so many things to do and plans to make!

Life goes on for Esther Del Vecchio.

"Losing our lovely home and possessions in the Oakland Hills firestorm in October 1991 was much more traumatic than losing a breast, but I have finally come to terms with it. We are happily back in our rebuilt home and hope to spend the rest of our lives here."

*I*n 1972, at the age of fifty-seven, I noticed that my left breast was getting a little heavier than my right. I didn't feel a lump, my breast just felt different somehow. One day I read a magazine article by Mrs. Birch Bayh about her breast cancer. My symptoms sounded exactly like hers. I immediately went to my doctor, who felt nothing but suggested I get a mammogram just to make sure.

The radiologist said the mammogram looked normal. When my internist phoned with the good news—"not to worry"—I told him I was concerned because it still didn't feel right. His answer to me was, "Keep your hands in your pockets and stop feeling!"

I decided to go on my own to a surgeon who had performed a biopsy on my right breast for a benign cyst six years earlier. He did a biopsy which showed a malignant tumor hidden behind a thickening of the breast. The next day I had a radical mastectomy,

I lost a breast, but it saved my life. I am now seventy-eight and in excellent health. My husband of fifty-six years has always been loving and caring and just happy to have me here and well.

He still thinks I'm beautiful.

Ruth J.
Oakland Hills, California

"There has been only one major change in my life since my diagnosis. As with most crises that come into your life, I began thinking about the things I had never done. I was fifty-two and believe it or not, the only thing I had never truly experienced was being a housewife. I graduated from high school on a Monday night in 1957 and went to work the next morning as a secretary. Except for a week off for the births of each of my three sons, I have worked every day since then.

When I first began work we desperately needed the money. But after thirty-five years, I worked simply because I had always worked. So I had never done the things a housewife does. I had never driven a car around town doing errands during the day, or been home when something exciting in the world was being broadcast on television, or done so many other little things that most people take for granted. In any case, nine months after my diagnosis, I resigned my position and came home.

Most housewives will probably think I'm a little crazy, but this is one of the most exciting times of my life. I clean my house during the day rather than during the night or on weekends. I go to the store during the day, not during the night. I do my laundry during the day and not during the night. My husband and I now have dinner at 5:30 P.M. each day instead of 7:30 P.M. It's a whole new world out there for me."

*T*he first thing that entered my mind when my surgeon told me my lump was malignant was the newsreel

27

where President Franklin D. Roosevelt made his famous speech stating, "We have nothing to fear but fear itself." I had almost no fear because I was familiar with the diagnosis and treatment of breast cancer due to the voracious reading I had done on the subject for so many years. Knowledge can win over many frightening things that happen to you in your lifetime.

When my gynecologist discovered a lump in my breast, it was because of my reading that I knew that it was probably malignant and that we had probably found it early. I simply did not feel that it had spread, and I was correct in this assumption. I was familiar with the various types of breast cancers, so when I was told by my surgeon that mine was infiltrating duct adenocarcinoma, I knew it was a "garden variety" type of breast cancer found in older women, and not the fast-spreading, more serious type of cancer.

I knew that the survival rate from having a lumpectomy or a mastectomy was the same and what treatment I wanted. Still, my surgeon was a little dumbfounded when I told him within five minutes of my diagnosis that I wanted a lumpectomy, axillary node dissection, radiation, and tamoxifen. He, the radiation oncologist, and the medical oncologist all agreed with my request, and this was what I did. Of course, this would not have been the case had the cancer been found to have spread. All this knowledge came into play on that fateful day.

My biopsy was performed nine days after my fifty-second birthday, and my lumpectomy was done the next day. On

Sunday morning I went home. Two weeks later I returned to work.

There were only two situations during the entire treatment and healing process that surprised me and for which I was not prepared. The first was the extent of damage to my right arm from having all my lymph nodes removed. After eleven months my right arm, from the shoulder/armpit area to the elbow, is still numb and swollen. The pain I had with it for about ten months has almost ceased, but the numbness and swelling continue to this day. This wouldn't bother me so much, but I am right-handed. The only two things I couldn't do during recuperation were running the vacuum and mash potatoes. After eleven months I have finally managed to do both. My arm problem was the most debilitating and painful part of the entire healing process.

The other surprise to me was the extent of the radiation treatments. Despite all my research, I had believed that you would be treated possibly two times a month for six months. Needless to say, I was surprised to learn that radiation treatments were once a day, every day, five days a week for six weeks. The treatments didn't affect me in any way. I went at 8:00 A.M. each day, and from there I went to work. I never missed a day's work.

My reason for writing this letter is to advise other women in no uncertain terms that they should do what I have done since my middle twenties: Find a good gynecologist with whom they can develop a good rapport and stay with him or her. I had been with my gynecologist for thirty-two years before the day of discovery of breast cancer. He knew me well, knew my body well, and knew that I had had a mammogram every year, which he had prescribed. I don't believe it's just going to a gynecologist every year that makes a difference. I believe that it's going to the same gynecologist every year that makes the difference. I had thirty-two years of gynecological records in one place and twelve years of mammograms in one place, so when the time came for me to go to my medical oncologist with my records there was absolutely no problem with locating and putting them together.

As I have stated, the breast cancer didn't upset me too much. I attacked it as I would any project given to me in my office. I laid out my medical schedules, radiation schedules, etc., and performed them. I didn't have time to think about the cancer problem—I was too busy taking care of it. I treated it as I would another business problem, and it worked for me. I am quite sure, however, that working at my office also helped me immensely because I didn't have time to think about anything else. With both my work and attending to my medical needs, my mind did not have time to get upset, worried, or depressed.

I must end this story by recognizing two people who helped me through this entire journey. First, my employer made it very clear to me on my first day back on the job that I was to make my own schedule. If I felt like staying in bed any day of the week and did not feel like coming to work, then I was to do so. If the radiation made me sick or fatigued and I didn't feel like working, then I was to stay at home. If I missed a whole month's work, he would not care—his only concern was my recuperating well and beating this thing called cancer. My employer's attitude was remarkable and lifted a very heavy burden from my shoulders.

Lastly, and most importantly, is my husband. To begin with, he is twenty years older than I, and he took my illness rather hard, although he tried not to show it. It would have seemed ironic to him that he would be seventy-two years old and alive, and I would be fifty-two years old and dead. He drove me to every medical appointment I had for four months. He took me to every radiation treatment. He even took me to the drugstore to purchase the tamoxifen. He bathed me after the surgery because of the drainage tube left in my side. He fed me and kept the house clean. He never left me. This attitude also was remarkable and lifted a very heavy burden from my shoulders. Between the two of us, we never once were depressed over our situation.

These men are two of the reasons I got through the entire episode of breast cancer with such ease. My worries and burdens were lifted through knowledge of the problem and wonderful people. I know that I am one of the luckiest people in the world for having been in my situation. I know many others are not as fortunate.

I see many happy years ahead of me. I am not concerned with a recurrence of breast cancer. Although I understand that 30 percent of the women who have a similar cancer to mine do have recurrences, I refuse to dwell on it. If it happens to me again, then I will simply attack it as I did the first time. I have no fear.

Judith O.
Beckley, West Virginia

"I will have my ninety-sixth birthday October 12."

*F*ive years ago I went to the doctor for my usual checkup. He found a small lump in my left breast. I decided to have it removed at once. The doctor was very thoughtful and only removed the lump, not the whole breast.

He also gave me Nolvadex tablets, which I took twice every day for three years. The prices started going up, so I asked if I might stop taking the tablets. He sent me to the hospital for an examination. There was no sign of cancer. That was more than two years ago. I am okay today and I am so grateful, I thought I might help somebody else.

My best thoughts to anyone who has cancer.

Mary M. Brittain
LaGrange Park, Illinois

Patty Andrew is twenty-eight years old.

I discovered a lump in my right breast while doing a monthly self-exam. I saw my gynecologist that same day and was told to "give it some time." That it would probably disappear after my menstrual period.

For ten long days I hoped I would wake up and the lump would be gone. (It wasn't.) I went back to the doctor and he referred me to a surgeon, who performed a needle aspiration. The surgeon was unsuccessful in retrieving any fluid or cells. He scheduled me for a biopsy the following week, but he reassured me it was a fibroid cyst. He said, "Breast cancer is extremely rare for someone your age. Go home and don't worry." But I was educated enough to know that cancerous tumors do not normally contain fluid. In my heart, I knew I was in serious trouble.

As soon as the surgeon examined the tumor in the operating room, he was convinced it was malignant. Cancerous tumors are graded, based on the pathologist's visual determination. My tumor was a grade III/III (the very worst).

Before my diagnosis I had been trying to get pregnant

with my second child. The day I was scheduled to start chemotherapy, I found out I was pregnant. My doctor felt it was extremely risky to carry to full-term because I wouldn't be able to undergo the chemotherapy. Therefore, my chances of remission would be very low. I also had to consider the fact that I have a five-year-old son and a husband who need me. After our discussion I made the decision to end the pregnancy.

The day of the termination was one of the saddest days of my life.

Because my tumor was small—1 cm—and the margins were clear of any cancerous cells, I was able to choose a lumpectomy, which would be followed by radiation after my six-month course of chemotherapy. I was on a combination of three chemotherapy drugs for the first two weeks of every month. The first round wasn't too bad, although my doctor informed me that it would get progressively worse. He also told me that I would lose my hair very rapidly, probably within the next week. Seven days after that appointment I was completely bald. It was very traumatic and very depressing.

In December, five days after I was released from the hospital for leukopenia (the chemo had destroyed most of my white blood cells and allowed infection to set in throughout my body), I lost my twenty-nine-year old brother to AIDS. My brother and I were very close and had been throughout our childhood. Watching him suffer and deteriorate to under eighty lbs. was one of the hardest things I've ever experienced. I thank God daily that he is no longer suffering and in pain. But I miss him terribly. I was both physically and emotionally exhausted at this point.

In March I completed my chemotherapy. After a bout of pneumonia my doctor decided it was best to forgo the last treatment. My body just could not tolerate any more "poison." I began my radiation in April. I was to receive thirty treatments, five days a week, for six weeks. I would then have to go to a larger facility to receive eight "booster" treatments, to treat the tumor bed.

On May 1st, I was convinced I was pregnant again. I had no physical signs—just my instinct. I truly thought this was a blessing! But again, my joy was short-lived. I saw five different doctors in five days, and I learned there are no studies to indicate how dangerous it is to become pregnant less than a month after chemotherapy (doctors strongly urge women to wait two years before becoming pregnant after chemotherapy). I was on a blood thinner (for a heart catheter in which they administered my chemo drugs), which was known to cause major birth defects. I had also received radiation. Of course, our main concern was the recurrence of cancer. Pregnancy is hormonally regulated, as is breast cancer. After discussing the situation my doctor urged me to, once again, interrupt the pregnancy. It was just too risky.

On June 1st, once again, I terminated my pregnancy. I had to deal with the same emotions as before—hurt, grief, sadness. But most of all, I was angry. Why was this happening to me? Was I such a bad person to deserve such heartbreak? I was overwhelmed with all of the sadness in my life. I felt God had let me down. We say that He never gives us more than we can handle, but I felt like the exception to the rule. And I was just so tired.

It was the love of my family and friends that helped me to see that life is worth living. This past year has been a nightmare for us, but if I've learned anything over the past year, it's that we can all survive this game of life as long as we have each other.

With love,
Patty Andrew
Fairfield, Ohio

I was diagnosed with breast cancer in July 1968, twenty-five years ago, during a routine medical checkup. Little was said about breast cancer in those days. There were no support groups, at least not in New Hampshire. The only two people I had known who had had it had both died. As the parent of young children, naturally I was very frightened. While experts make much of self-examination, even after I knew I had a problem I still could not feel it.

The agreement was that the surgeon would do a biopsy while I was under anesthesia and, if the biopsy showed cancer, they would remove my breast. This is what happened. I had a radical mastectomy but neither chemotherapy nor radiation therapy afterwards. I recuperated fairly quickly, and returned to my high school teaching position for the next 15 years until my retirement.

Any bout with cancer makes one realize how precarious life is. As a result, each day has become infinitely precious to me because it means a day spent with my family. A sunset, the smell of apple blossoms, lunch with a friend—events I had always taken so lightly are now treasured. Petty annoyances are thrust aside. I no longer let trivialities bother me. In the classroom, I used the same philosophy and earned the respect and affection of my students. I never got angry or out of control. Any misbehavior, I could handle with a cool head and an understanding heart. (Kids have their "cancers," too.)

As I look back, I know that, despite the trauma I felt at the time, my experience with breast cancer truly enriched my life. I value family and friendships and the peace that has permeated my life ever since. I look back with gratitude to God for the wonderful life I have enjoyed—a tremendously rewarding career, a fifty-year marriage, four marvelous children, ten fantastic grandchildren, lovely siblings and siblings-in-law, and, yes, even a nice cat.

There is truly life after breast cancer.

Sincerely,
Alma L.
Manchester, New Hampshire

Jean Maynard was forty-four when she wrote this three years ago. She worked as a medical technologist in a hospital in Michigan. Her cancer turned out to be ductal carcinoma in situ contained in a five millimeter lesion. *"I was lucky."*

$\mathcal{A}$s to the idea of considering myself a "breast cancer survivor," I have a hard time with that concept. I feel that the term *survivor* is being overused to the point of losing impact, such as in the buzzwords "paradigm," "empowerment," and "down-sizing." I also feel that the term *survivor* after any situation implies, at some level, a deference or special treatment due the individual as a result of the experience. In fact, I feel that we are all survivors of something every day that we wake up. If it isn't breast cancer, it's accidents, old age, poverty, joblessness, or any other condition of the human race. I don't want to be singled out or made an example of or commended because of my behavior during a crisis or a lifetime. The behaviors that make breast cancer survivors are the same behaviors that make survivors in any situation. The things that helped me are the same things that help other survivors as well.

Needless to say, cancer has a tendency to cause an emphasis on the spiritual and religious aspects of life. Most prudent people, when they feel death is imminent, have a tendency to want to cover all the bases; and I was no exception. As a "returned" Catholic, I had been a regular church attendee but had a tendency to catch up on sleep or simply phase out when things got a little dull.

I suddenly found myself paying attention. I sought out the hospital chapel on work breaks. I appealed for delivery from fear. I knew I had to make the right decisions for the right reasons to accomplish my personal agenda, and that fear could disrupt that.

My short-term goal was to go on vacation out west in August. My midrange goal was to get my son married to a girl of my (oops! *his*) choice. My long-range goal was to have at least ten good years of retirement to spend with my husband Mike without work or illness interfering. Sometimes, I just want to cry. Offers of prayers began arriving. My mother had her club friends, aqua-aerobics group, and a convent of nuns pray for me. That's a group of experienced pray-ers! I could feel the psychic buildup of energy.

I am much closer to my fellow employees now than before. I know how awkward it is to talk to people who have just received bad news. My co-workers did exactly the right thing. They said they heard the news, they didn't know what to say, and they asked questions. By talking about it, I was able to become more objective and rational, and hopefully also helped educate people along the way. I've had a tendency to think that, sometimes, people are merely "work friends," but I found that many of these people are my true friends and feel enriched indeed.

You have to want to live. Those individuals deemed most obnoxious about getting their way are probably the most likely to establish control and ultimately live. I'll bet my mother never realized that those same qualities that made me a difficult child were the same qualities that were pointed out to me as my assets during cancer!

When problems arise educate yourself as much as you possibly can and ask questions. Write them down. Call people back if you forgot to ask. Ask where to get additional information on your condition. Get second and third opinions. Ask other people what they did when they were in your situation. Listen to your inner voice and follow your instinct. You know yourself better than anyone else. Leave *nothing* to chance. "S__ happens," as they say, and even the best doctors and hospitals may overlook or forget something. *You* must take control of your situation. Don't let anyone talk you into something with which you don't feel comfortable.

Cry whenever you feel like it. You'll probably cry at weird things. In my case, it was while dressing at the YMCA after swimming my laps. I finally realized that this was the last week I would be tucking that breast into a bra. I cried a good part of the day. It doesn't mean you made a bad decision. It just means that you are feeling bad.

Prepare for surgery like an athletic event, which, in most cases, it is, to some degree. In my case, I swam laps, tapered off cigarettes, and then quit the few days before both surgeries so that oxygenation during surgery would be maximal.

Get the best doctors, surgeons, and anesthesiologists

available. You are entrusting them with your life; and, before you do that, you have to trust them and have confidence in their abilities. My "flying" paranoia is exceeded only by my "anesthesia" paranoia. I had implicit trust in my surgeon. He didn't know it, but when he was called in as the surgeon on critical cases, I often was responsible for providing the cross-matched blood and blood products for his patients. Over the years I knew that he operated with minimal blood loss to the patients. He was quick, and his patients did not go back for repairs. I also knew that he was calm and, in turn, calmed those around him. When I met with him, he was patient and answered my questions respectfully. He did not impose his opinions on me. He did not question my decision. As there had been some possible anesthesia-related problems in my family, I expressed my concerns and anxiety to him and asked him to select the anesthesiologist he felt most comfortable with in the event of unforeseen problems. This was a *big* stretch of trust for me! In the meantime I ran around and rustled up my mother's anesthesia records as well as my own. Both the surgeon and the anesthesiologist were respectful of my concerns and treated them as valid. Talk to people. If you're afraid, tell them. People will understand.

Pray if you're comfortable with that. Meditate or do relaxation exercises. Read inspirational stories of people who beat the odds. Don't hang around negative people or events. You have enough of your own during these events.

Do something comforting for yourself. In my case I would take myself to the Cappuccino Café for a coffee mocha, topped with a mound of whipped cream and shaved chocolate. Who cares about cholesterol when you think you're going to die anyway? I'd bring a book and read by myself in a corner. The managers and employees of the café always seemed to transmit a positive energy (this is another thing you think you become an expert on when you think you're going to die!), and the caffeine buzz would give me a pickup.

While I was recovering from the mastectomy, I went several times a week. In fact, the day I got home from the hospital, Mike brought me a mocha from the café because he knew it made me feel good. I think this place deserves some of the credit for my recovery!

Exercise. Once you get the okay from your physician, do whatever you are capable of. A few endorphins go a long way. I was given the okay to swim again a little short of two weeks postsurgery. I swam laps every day. It wasn't a pretty sight initially, but it got better every day. Within three to four weeks, I had essentially 100 percent mobility on my affected side. I coincidentally worked off all the coffee mochas, too!

Ask for supportive thoughts to help you make the right decisions. Seek out people who have been in similar situations and get their input. Keep in mind that there is often no right or wrong decision in these cases, which is the best and worst aspect of breast cancer. Sometimes you just want someone else to tell you what to do. You know yourself and what works for you. Don't be afraid to fly in the face of convention. In my case lumpectomy with radiation was recommended. In my opinion, with my family history and a variety of other factors, I felt a mastectomy was more appropriate. I would not, however, be so presumptuous as to suggest that my decision would be the best thing for someone else in the same situation. Don't do anything quickly. In most cases you have weeks or even months from lump to surgery/radiation.

Don't be afraid to rock the boat if things aren't going the way you think they should. If I hadn't rocked the boat about my original lump and gotten someone to aspirate it, my outcome could have been very different. Somehow it had gotten overlooked in the concern over the calcifications. Reach out and support others. I feel I owe a lot of prayers and a lot of favors, and I'm doing my best to repay.

Live and enjoy every single day. I always have, and this hasn't changed my outlook. After I awoke after surgery the day of the mastectomy I watched the sunset from my hospital room window that night. I thanked God that I had the opportunity to see it. The loss of a breast does not cause the sun to stop rising or setting.

Love your family. Help them to be informed, too. They are also afraid at some level. God bless Mike for bringing me *Dr. Susan Love's Breast Book* and for supporting me at every step of the way. He was there when I cried and stepped back when I needed space. He loves me in spite of my tattered body with the mastectomy, C-section, and appendectomy scars. I guess I'm at the age now where I look better from the back than the front!

I thank God for my son, a fifteen-year-old who managed

to continue to treat me as all teenagers do their mothers at this stage of life! It helps keep you grounded in reality. I know that he had fears, and I know that I was prayed for and loved by him even though he wasn't always able to tell me. Unfortunately for him, it looks like I'll be around for a long time to continue to be the bane of his existence!

Because I feel that I did everything I could for myself, and I trusted when I couldn't, I am at peace with myself. I don't often think about not having a breast except when I change my clothes. I remember it like an old friend and go on with my life. I don't look back. I am not in fear of the future. If I have a recurrence or another cancer, so be it. I am confident I will do the best I can as I did this time.

I am not in denial. I am in Life.

Jean Maynard
Haslett, Michigan

I am a forty-one-year-old African-American woman. In August of 1990 my mother and I moved to Irving, Texas, with the company she works for. In September of 1991, I was diagnosed with breast cancer; and again in May of 1994. Both times I had a modified radical mastectomy. I was fortunate both times because I didn't need chemotherapy or radiation.

Emotionally, I still feel as if I'm on a roller coaster. Some days are up and some are down. I think the worst for me is slowing down and realizing that I can no longer work at my usual fast pace. I'm reading a lot now about creative and innovative approaches toward prevention of breast cancer. And I'm on a vegetarian diet, which I supplement with whole food vitamins, minerals, antioxidants, and herbs. I exercise thirty minutes a day three times a week. Lower stress with quiet breathing and meditating twice a week. I listen to talk and self-help and newsworthy radio programs daily, and I read more humorous books.

Overall, I'm living and learning holistically. As for the future, I plan to take long walks in the park, be less critical of myself, and if possible, return to college to complete my degree. I will create more nutritious meals, visit my local seacoasts in Texas, and, of course, I'll be playing my $1 each week in the Texas Lottery.

Plain and simple, just enjoying life to its fullest!

Sincerely,
Myra G.
Irving, Texas

Lois Joy Gabriel is a breast cancer activist who lives in Underhill, Vermont. She wrote this letter to an "on-line" friend, Susan.

"Susan had sent me a copy of an article about herself which appeared in her local paper. The article told of her personal experience with breast cancer and her determination to beat the disease. Shortly after the article appeared, Susan's cancer recurred, She wrote me and said she was feeling down and that she felt like a failure. This is a copy of my reply to her. To some, it may appear a bit on the dark side, but as you know, living with breast cancer has many sides. Some days are very dark and very difficult; others are joyous and bright. All are very real to the woman living with breast cancer, and are filled with hidden gifts and true miracles."

Dear Susan,
I cried when I read your story. You and I have so many parallels in our lives—loving husbands, an adored child, supportive friends. We are very blessed. My heart broke when you told about life before breast cancer. Your words, "It was a good life," have been my words. When I think back on my life before breast cancer I grieve, too. I also had been given a "good life," one filled with so many gifts. Then one day I walked into a doctor's office and was run over by a train. Now I am forever changed. And although there are many days when I feel so much more alive

and more aware of all of life than I ever was before I had cancer, I still carry this very deep grief and sadness. I don't think it will ever go away.

I haven't had a recurrence so I don't know what it is like to walk in your shoes. But I do know that this disease touches us all so intimately, and I think I can understand why you feel you have failed. It has nothing to do with cancer, but with an old notion that women have to be perfect. Somewhere deep inside we still believe it. We suffer from that curse, even striving to be the perfect breast cancer survivor! Even when our lives are threatened, we feel we can never make a mistake, never falter.

The truth is that the responsibility for beating cancer was never yours to begin with. It has always belonged to our government and the medical research establishment, which for years and years now have continued to fail women.

You know, I have a lot of trouble with that expression, "beating cancer." I know people mean well when they say "you can beat this thing," but it places an awfully heavy burden on those of us who already have enough to bear. The responsibility for conquering cancer needs to be placed where it belongs—with the people who have the power to do it. I wonder if anyone in Washington has a heart! Within me is a spirit that rages and shakes its fist. I want to say: *You* beat the damn cancer! *You* are the people we pay to find a cure for this disease. *You*, in the Congress, and *you* at the NIH! You have *our* money! We are trusting you to do your job. I have a ten-year-old to mold into a loving, moral human being, and God only knows if I will have enough time to do it! But at least *I'm doing my job!*" Sometimes I shake my fist because I know I am right, and sometimes I shake my fist because I feel helpless.

God, Susan, just look at our world. Actors and athletes make multimillions of dollars for a few month's work; children starve to death. Almost a thousand a week lose their mothers to breast cancer. We live in a place where the government will not make finding a cure for cancer a national priority but will get involved in a baseball strike! Where is the sanity here?

I'm forty-six years old and breast cancer has been killing women my entire life. I remember being a child and one day finding my mother crying. When I asked her what was wrong she told me that her friend had cancer and that they had to remove her breast. I remember feeling so frightened at the thought that such a thing as removing a breast really happened. I guess my mother saw my distress because she quickly wiped her tears away and smiled and said. "It's okay. By the time you grow up it will be cured." I know she really believed it, too. It was the 50's; the future was bright and hopeful. Now that I have had both my breasts removed, I wonder if my mother remembers that day. We have never spoken about it. I'm afraid that if I remind her, it might break her heart, knowing that she made a promise to me that was never kept.

Susan, if you look into your heart, you will know that you are not a failure. You are strong and smart, and you have a loving spirit which you shared with others when you stood up and spoke out. I'm proud of you.

May God's peace heal you all over,

Love,
Lois

$\mathcal{I}$ *was* a farmer's wife all my life. I had five children, and when the youngest one started kindergarten I went to work at an implement company near my home. This made it possible for me to come home during my lunch hour and fix lunch for six or seven people. Since we were farmers, this had to be a substantial meal.

In March of 1977 I went to the doctor for my checkup and mentioned a red patch under my left breast. He sent me to a surgeon, who thought it was some form of skin cancer and scheduled surgery to remove it. They did the surgery on Tuesday, found out it was malignant on Wednesday, and scheduled a mastectomy on Thursday. The cancer was in almost all of the lymph nodes that they removed. They gave me radiation, which affected my throat and made it impossible to swallow food. I sipped milkshakes for several weeks. I also received burns under my arm. I started on exercises right away, but it was impossible for me to reach up and back. After the radiation two years of chemotherapy were planned for me.

My chances of surviving were not very good.

A year later, in February of 1978, my husband came home from driving the school bus and suffered a fatal heart attack. At the time we were farming 600 acres for two elderly landladies. I decided to continue farming for them with the help of a trusted employee and my sons. I had planned never to date or marry again, but plans get changed. I remarried in June 1981. I gained four more daughters and ten grand-children. We certainly have big dinners on Thanksgiving and Christmas.

My left arm is still quite a bit bigger than my right one, and I still can't reach up or back, but no one even notices it.

I'm just happy to be alive.

Evelyn G.
Rossville, Indiana

hank you for this chance to tell my story. My name is Cathy Jo Gove. I have been married for twenty-one years to Doug and have a twelve-year-old daughter, Rianne Jo. I am forty years old and I have breast cancer. Here's how this all came about:

On my thirty-ninth birthday, March 25, 1992, I had my first mammogram. No sweat. Everything came back normal. I wasn't surprised. I've never had any sort of female problems. No family history of cancer. Ate right. Not overweight. Had not been on birth control for about fourteen years. I had my daughter at twenty-eight and breastfed her. I had only been in the hospital once in my life, for a C section when Rianne Jo was born.

Fast-forward to October 1992. While doing my self-exam during my bath I found a large lump on the left side of my left breast. Where did this come from? It was not there the week before. Within the next two weeks I saw my primary physician and a surgeon, had another mammogram and needle biopsy done. Mind you, this was not a pea-size lump, but a lump large enough to grab hold of. Still I wasn't too concerned. I felt I was in very capable hands and it would turn out to be something minor. In other words, I didn't worry myself sick over this. On November 2, 1992, I had a biopsy. Bad news. Cancer. The following Monday, November 9, I had a mastectomy done on my left breast. They removed a 3.8cm lump and of twenty-two lymph nodes taken, twelve had cancer. In a matter of eight months my life was changed forever.

Am I bitter? No way! I'm alive!!!

Next step: "Chemotherapy." My husband, my sister Linda, and I met with an oncologist and were told what my chemo would consist of. Very aggressive chemo was decided on because of several factors: my young age, good health (other than the cancer), and the fact that the cancer was aggressive, having gone into so many lymph nodes. My attitude was "Do whatever needs to be done."

Had my first chemotherapy session Dec. 3, 1992. One week before Christmas I was out shopping and my hair started falling out. I had my husband shave my head that weekend. Now I'm not a vain person but I cried—for the first time. Having no hair was worse than no breast because people knew by looking at me that something was wrong. I didn't want anyone feeling sorry for me.

Wigs were very annoying, so I started wearing scarves and hats. (Boy, am I sick of hats!) This is when I knew that some people were uncomfortable being around me. People at my job (more men than women) did not want to see me as a constant reminder that we are all vulnerable. I took a six-month leave from my job to get through chemo. Six months of being sick, tired, bald, and fat. Yes, fat! I put on twenty-five pounds during my chemo. How depressing. I had my last session on May 10. Party time!!

I have *slowly* started to lose my extra weight (not fast

enough for me). My hair has come back in curly (it was straight as a board before), and was I really this gray before? Thank goodness for hair color! Even my eyelashes came back longer than before. My hair is about an inch all around and back to my dark brown, so I took the next big step. No more hats. Oh sure, I get my share of looks, but that's okay. I made it this far, a few funny looks don't get to me anymore.

So, that's my story. No different than I'm sure a lot of stories. What a wonderful lesson I have learned through all this. Slow down, enjoy yourself, love your family more. They are so special. Without them I don't think I could have been so strong. My husband told me the other night I was the bravest person he has ever met. I told him it had nothing to do with being brave, just with wanting to live and be the best person I can be.

I hope my story gives hope to others. Breast cancer is not a death sentence. We will survive!

Love,
Cathy Jo Gove
Newbury Park, California

I have just settled a malpractice suit against the radiologist who had treated me continuously for four years prior to my breast cancer surgery. I feel free now to discuss the situation since I have accepted a settlement. I chose not to go to trial.

The doctor made a mistake in judgment for two years. Prior breast surgery left scars on my breast and one was changing as I watched it. It was thickening. The radiologist told me that cancer did not grow in scar tissue—"so don't worry." Of course, she was wrong. At a pre-trial hearing my lawyer asked why I wasn't referred for a biopsy when the thickening was first noticed. The doctor's answer haunted me. "We can't biopsy everyone . . . we would be doing too many biopsies. Many would not be necessary."

This doctor played God with my life. I really had hoped that I didn't have a case. But when experts looked at my X rays they acknowledged my inner fears. Instead of sending me for a biopsy in 1991, she should have sent me in 1989!

From this I have learned the following:

1. Women should go to more than one doctor to look at their X rays if there is the slightest hint of a problem.

2. Women should listen to their inner thoughts. My doctor made me feel like I was overreacting when I ques-

tioned her judgment in 1989. She told me I had to have faith in her. It was my mistake that I didn't follow through on my inner feelings. But when a respected doctor tells you not to worry, "You're fine. Come back in a year," you walk out of the office floating on a cloud.

3. Biopsy—biopsy—biopsy. It's the only way to really tell if something is malignant or not.

My story is not over. My husband and I are snowbirds. When we reached Florida this November I went to a surgeon I respected. I have cystic breasts and he found loads of lumps and bumps in my remaining breast and he biopsied two of them. He understood all my fears about the cancer returning in my remaining breast. He asked me how I would feel about having a simple mastectomy on my remaining breast, since he needed to perform two biopsies on the breast and when he finished, he felt there would be very little breast left. I felt this was right for me to do.

Well, good news—the lumps were benign. Still, I followed my heart and am now breast-less.

But I am at peace.

Sincerely,
Ellen B.
Delray Beach, Florida

In December of 1967 I discovered a lump in my left breast. I was thirty years old.

Scared and upset, I went to the doctor. He told me I had to have a biopsy and, if it was malignant, my breast would have to be removed. I had two boys. David was seven and Danny, thirteen. I didn't want their Christmas holidays ruined, so I asked the doctor to let me wait until after Christmas. Against his better judgment, he finally agreed.

I had the biopsy on the 9th of January, 1968. The report came back positive. The doctors took me back to the operating room and removed my breast. I was not given any follow-up treatment.

One year and three months later, I had a recurrence. I thought surely I would never live to see my young children grow up. I prayed to God to please let me live to raise them. My husband was by my side all the way. Nights I couldn't sleep, he would hold me close and tell me everything would be all right. His love for me gave me strength and courage to keep fighting.

The doctors removed my ovaries and I had a series of radiation treatments. *They gave me a year to live.*

Well, it's been twenty-five years! With God's help I beat the cancer! I've seen my children grow up and become happily married. I'm a beautician, and am still working.

My life was spared. My prayer is that a cure for cancer can be found and that every woman who has breast cancer can be as fortunate as I have been.

Sincerely yours,
Nell Harvell
Arab, Alabama

*I*n 1963, when I was 32, a bride of thirteen years, and my children were 2 ½, 4, 8, 12, I found a mass in my breast. A biopsy was performed. A few days later, when the stitches were removed and no report had come back, the consensus was that all was well. However, in a day or two, there came a devastating phone call. The doctors wanted to talk to both my husband and me. We knew the inevitable.

They told me I would need radical surgery. For a while, I lost the desire to live. But then they told us my chances were fifty-fifty. When I heard that, I began to cling to the fact that my odds were as good as not to survive, and I was determined and ready to cope.

Seeing my children grow, participating in their school functions, going through the teenage years, and planning and attending all four weddings was a special privilege to me. My husband and I continue to have a wonderful life. And my life-long dream of becoming an artist has come true.

In 1983, I thought it would be wonderful to again have a more normal body and opted for a breast reconstruction. Yes, I have the controversial Dow Corning implant. I have had no ill effects and am very satisfied with the way it responds to fondling (like my own breast). I've had anxious moments, hearing all the negative reports. My doctors tell me the implant problems are 2% of the many who have done this procedure. I am sorry for the unhappiness those women have experienced. My heart goes out to them. I hope the 98% continue to do fine.

As for myself, I feel truly blessed.

Sincerely,
Jane M. Gehring
Moundridge, Kansas

Anne Kirchheimer, forty-three, is an artist and a writer. She wrote this just as her treatment was coming to an end.

*G*etting a breast cancer diagnosis, then going through surgery, radiation, and chemotherapy is a mental and physical feat akin to participating in a grueling sporting event. One more month to go on chemo and I will have broken the ribbon. Crowds won't be there cheering, judges won't be crowning me with a wreath. Still, I'll feel like a winner and my friends and family will share in the glory. They are my coaches, my fan club, my trainers, lovingly pushing me on when I say I can't take it anymore, when I want to quit.

And those thoughts come often, especially while on chemotherapy. The journal I've been keeping can attest to that.

Three days after chemo and the temperature outside has hit four below zero. Enough to rock the core of any normal human being. On top of that, my stomach feels as if it contains a piece of lead the size of a bowling ball. Between the cold weather and the terrible stomachache, I wonder how I am going to make it through this.

It takes perseverance to plod through this odyssey that started in mid-July, when a lump was discovered during a routine gynecological visit.

Every ounce of energy has gone to fight for my health and to take care of my two small sons. While in radiation I could never figure out if the bone-deep fatigue came from the treatment or the unrelenting motion of Joseph and Kenny.

Help with the kids came from those close to me, but added understanding came from the other women also waiting for their daily radiation treatment. Some days, when the machine broke down, the wait would be for hours, and we would always chat. We'd commiserate on fatigue, our skin irritation, and laugh about our concern over body odor, not being able to shave under the arm or use deodorant. We'd talk about how radiation was a breeze compared to chemo. For me they were like a support group. They gave a boost to my morale, understanding how tough it is, taking care of two small kids while going through treatment, a divorce, and a relocation.

I didn't write about it in my journal, but I can clearly remember the sunny August day when I got the first piece of bad news. The lab results on what was believed to be an aspirated cyst came out cancerous. After hanging up the telephone, I burst into tears. What came to mind was the movie *Terms of Endearment*, and the dying mother of small children saying her good-byes.

Numb is the only way to describe my state of mind during the next month, which was crammed with doctor visits, a biopsy, a lymph node operation, results, second opinions, and decisions. Ellen, my sister, my mother, and my girlfriends accompanied me through this medical maze. They became my ears, relaying doctors' comments to me when I cried or became too numb to hear.

The ups and downs are wrenching. "It's a small tumor, you may not even need radiation," reported the breast surgeon in her positive, upbeat manner. The next call: The bad news is, two of the thirteen lymph nodes we removed showed cancer. You'll need chemotherapy, as well as radiation.

"The good news is you do not need a mastectomy."

We all have the different hells we have to go through. Men go through wars. Vietnam must sure have been hell to go through. No one in this world will be lucky enough to miss some form of hell.

Oh God . . . how will I do it? Here I am living alone with a six-year-old and a three-year-old and I have to go through this.

And the question is: How long is "this" going to continue?

Before starting chemo treatments, a patient must sign a form stating that she understands that there is a small percentage of a chance that chemotherapy treatments for breast cancer can cause leukemia, kidney or bladder disease. Still another worry.

Some days I don't feel that powerful. The challenge is to be able to give a measure of security to two small children during an insecure time. My oldest son instinctively took on the role of strong male in the household. This new behavior, somewhat bossy and controlling, affected him adversely with playmates in his new school. He was only seven at the time and needed to be a kid, not carry the burdens of adulthood.

The youngest became scared and depressed merely from the sight of bandages on my hand or arm, a result of the great search for a noncollapsed vein during chemo IVs. Our pediatrician recommended short-term crisis intervention therapy for him. He was only three-and-a-half years old. Cancer is another one of those family diseases. It affects everyone. All we could do was trudge on, each of us coping as best we could.

Today I feel burnt out. Up all night with Joseph, who had a high fever and was throwing up. In the middle of the night Kenny arrived in my bed, too. I was squeezed in the middle of the two of them, one dizzy and burning with fever, the other coughing continuously. I prayed, "Please don't let me get sick." I felt like a lab animal waiting to get zapped with the experimental virus, but today, other than being burnt out on children, illness, raging fever, I feel OK.

In January I was hospitalized for a week with pneumonia during my low immunity period that results from chemotherapy.

I can't settle down and sleep. I was worried all night about my little boys. How am I supposed to give them the security and happiness they need, if I am constantly having a health crisis? How much anxiety about my health can Joseph, six, tolerate? I feel that I am failing him as a mother because I can't get myself well.

Joe is such a little man. Last night, when he put on an apron and compulsively started drying the dishes, it broke my heart. What could be going on in the poor little guy's mind? He takes such responsibility. I hope to hell I am well and strong by the summer so we can just have a ball. They deserve it. Let's pray for strength and health for the boys and me. I can't leave them now. They need me. They feel secure with me despite this health mess.

No matter how surrounded and supported we are, we remain ultimately alone to face the sickness, take the treatment, and confront the underlying fear of death. I quickly discovered that "one day at a time" is not just a motto for sober alcoholics. If I couldn't do a day at a time, I'd settle for fifteen minutes.

What's hard is feeling physically fine, even with cancer careening around in my body, then submitting to chemotherapy and feeling horrendous. Then by the time I'm feeling better, it's time for another dose. It's terrifying to submit to having poison shot into your body. Someone is always asking me what the prognosis is. And it seems the New Age people are asking me if I really should be doing chemo at all. I don't know. Nobody does. I guess now it's an act of faith. I made the decision to go for chemo, but the results are now with a higher power. I know there are no guarantees.

Life is an unknown—take it day by day.

Ann Kirchheimer

$\mathcal{I}$ *am* an eighty-seven-year-old cancer survivor, thank God.

In 1963 (thirty years ago!), I had surgery for the removal of my left breast. My left arm had been swelling, and my breast felt hard and was draining. Why, you may wonder, didn't I suspect there was something serious? I was too busy! My husband was ill, and I was teaching a heavy load with evening classes to boot! It was a fellow teacher who noticed my swollen arm and insisted I see my doctor. The doctor ordered me into the hospital *that day* and prepared me for surgery the next day.

My breast and all the nodes were removed. This was followed by thirty-six radiation treatments. Just three months later he advised me to have the other breast removed, too. I was a long time healing, and to this day I suffer from the radiation burns. But I have lived a full life. I always realized that cancer could rise again and I'd better make my days count.

I have been so lucky—my children have become successful citizens, and I was able to care for my husband to his last days—and happy days they were. I continued teaching until I was seventy-eight and then headed the Literacy Program, receiving several commendations.

Cancer is an ogre! But it need not break your spirit. God

may not see fit to heal, but he never forsakes us; and, if we are willing to try, He gives us the courage to go on *living* 'til our last breath.

Yours sincerely,
Mary C.
Indianapolis, Indiana

No one chooses cancer. I have become another statistic—one in every nine women diagnosed with cancer. I am also a one-year survivor. I was diagnosed with noninvasive intraductal adenocarcinoma following my third biopsy.

When the oncologist called to give me the results of the tests his words were foreign. But within 24 hours I had become an expert on discussing types of breast cancer and various forms of treatment. If I had to face this dreadful disease, I would at least face it head on with all the facts available to the lay person. I had to make choices, and I wanted to make them quickly. If I was to give it the most challenging fight of my life, I wanted to be totally prepared.

My choices were these: to do nothing, to have a lumpectomy with radiation, to participate in a nationwide research study with drugs, or to have a total mastectomy. The margins surrounding the lump were clear, but they were very narrow. Not enough surrounding tissue had been removed with the lump to guarantee me that the entire cancer had been removed. And so I wasn't comfortable with doing nothing more. At the time I was working full-time and in college four nights a week and did not have the time or energy required to go through the six weeks of radiation therapy. Also, as my research soon revealed, radiation treatment comes with its own drawbacks.

Every direction I turned offered choices, forcing me to put my priorities in their proper place, and make decisions. The nationwide study that is being conducted with tamoxifen included the radiation therapy and, therefore, it seemed out of the question for me. Although I would like to have the added security of the tamoxifen fighting any cells that may have left the area of the breast, it was only offered as part of the study. My life was so totally full and active that I consequently chose to have a mastectomy. As severe as that choice may seem to others, it would provide me with the peace of mind that the cancerous cells were gone.

I am not so naive as to think that none of the cancerous cells could have left the area and attached themselves to another area or organ of my body. No one could guarantee me that. However, statistics show that there is a 99 percent success rate when mastectomies are the selected treatment for noninvasive breast cancers. That is a figure that is difficult to argue with.

I am the first to acknowledge that mastectomy is not for everyone. I can only offer to anyone who is faced with this choice to do as much research as possible before making a decision. Make the choice that you can live with. I took the most dramatic treatment available. If the cancer returns, I will know that I did everything in my power to conquer it. I will not look back and say, "I wish I had done more." I did the most I could. With my decision, I vowed I would never look back. I have not. I look forward. I have given it the good fight.

My oncologist has already told me that the same conditions exist in my remaining breast. If I am diagnosed with cancer in that breast, I know it will be a new cancer. It will not have spread from one breast to the other. I will also know that I can survive. I will ultimately make the decision to have that breast removed also. My only regret, as I reflect back, is that I didn't have them both removed at the same time. However, I have discovered that I am an extremely strong person. I will face whatever life offers. I will play out the hand I've been dealt. If anyone can beat this most dreaded of diseases, I am confident it is me.

Sincerely.
Rose Frank
Livingston, New Jersey

I am writing this letter to give hope to others. I am eighty-two years young and this is the thirtieth year since my right breast was radically removed by Dr. Jerome Urban at the Memorial Hospital in New York City. Dr. Urban never approved of breast implants, and so I've been wearing a bra prosthesis, comfortably, for all this time. I continue to go for a breast examination at least once a year and have had no further problems with having one breast. It was early detection and early action that saved me. The three steps to full recovery are: 1) Run, do not walk, to the nearest mammogram center. 2) Do not delay necessary surgery. 3) Do not panic. It takes hope, love, and caring people to pull you through.

> With kindest regards,
> Belle Panzer
> Margate, Florida

Just days back home from a marvelous trip to Europe with my husband I was slapped in the face by reality when a call from my gynecologist informed me that some abnormality had shown up in the mammogram I had done before I went away. She recommended a biopsy, which I calmly scheduled for the following week. After all, cancer was something that happened to other people, not to me.

The frozen section showed no malignancy. So for the next week all I chanted was, "Thank you, God." But my joy at having escaped was short-lived.

I went to my surgeon's office, alone, a week later to have my stitches removed. And it was there that he gave me the bad news. The permanent section showed intraductal carcinoma.

Suddenly, I was thrust into a nightmare. *I had cancer! I had breast cancer!* In the course of just the next few minutes I heard the words mastectomy, reconstructive surgery, oncologists . . . Then, at that very moment, not knowing whether I would live or die, I made a very conscious decision. I would handle the entire cancer ordeal with grace, style, and dignity. I was determined to be like Grace Kelly . . . cool, calm, collected. For some reason, this was very important to me.

Let me tell you, before cancer, I didn't cry over spilled

milk, I yelled! I hovered to see if the children loaded the dishwasher right, got easily annoyed if my husband didn't do a task fast enough, even counted the items in the basket of the shopper ahead of me in the express line. Cancer changed all that, permanently, thank goodness. Today I live life one day at a time in a mellow rather than manic pace. And, following my lead, we've become a kinder and gentler family.

Even though I'm just a housewife and mother (not a celebrity in any form), I'd like to offer some important thoughts. Early detection is vital to saving your life. Mammograms and self-exams for the women and prostate exams for the men in their lives are key. My own cancer was detected so early that, even though I made the decision to have my breast removed, I had a very high chance at survival from the start. As for the loss of a breast, truly, for me, that was no big deal. I have lived all these years with an extra thirty or forty pounds on my body and it's never bothered me. So the removal of a few pounds of tissue sure isn't going to get me down.

The most wonderful part is that I'm alive and, at this point in time, have been pronounced cancer-free. Applause . . . CANCER-FREE!

Astrid M.
Crystal Beach, Florida

Merle Clark sent this poem in November, 1994.

I know of the terror
in the black night
the loneliness
just when you thought you were "fine."

I remember the anger
when I should have felt blessed
when loved ones tried their best
when I looked in the mirror.

The feminist in me said "So what!"
The women in me wept—again and again.
The child in me wanted my life to be
the way it was before . . .

Now the black velvet nights glitter with stars.
The tears are not for me, but for my sister,
because her journey is not yet complete.

Today I feel blessed . . . and beautiful!
Proud, defiant, and at peace
at last.

It will come.
It will come, dear sister . . .
I know.

Merle Clark—diagnosed September 1991

77

This poem arrived in November 1995.

AGAIN

The cancer came back
>*but I can still walk*
>*run*
>*and dance!*

Now that the sadness is gone
>*I still laugh*
>*love*
>*and make music.*

My world tumbled down . . . again.

But I can rebuild
>*relearn*
>*and go forward*
this time without fear.

Merle Clark
July 1995

I *was* thirty-three years old and nine months pregnant when I was diagnosed with breast cancer. I found the lump while I was in the shower. I was doing a self-exam and a massage to stimulate my milk ducts for breast feeding. My baby was due on July 28 and, since this was to be my last child, I had planned to breast-feed for the first time.

When I went to my doctor for my weekly prenatal checkup I mentioned the lump to him. He examined it very carefully and said he'd like to do a mammogram. I was concerned because a mammogram might harm the baby, but my doctor assured me it was okay because the baby was already fully developed. The mammogram showed a lot of calcification around the lump and it was suggested I see a surgeon and have it removed and biopsied right away. At this point I was not only concerned for my unborn child, but for myself.

On July 9 my baby was put on monitors and I was put under general anesthesia. I had a biopsy. When I woke up in the recovery room my surgeon was on one side of me and my obstetrician was on the other. I heard one of them say, "I have some bad news." The nurses later told me that everyone in recovery was crying.

We decided to begin treatment as soon as possible. On July 21, my 10 pound 8 ounce baby boy was born. The next day I was taken into the operating room for breast surgery. I couldn't wait to see my new baby that night. The joy and love I felt just holding him and feeding him made me almost forget what I had just gone through!

My oncologist suggested six months of chemotherapy and six weeks of radiation. I had all of the normal concerns about side effects such as nausea, hair loss, and fatigue. After all, I had three small children to look after. But I managed. I would take my daughter, then nine years old, to school every morning and then, with my four-year-old son and new baby in tow, I went for radiation treatments—five days a week for six weeks.

On the days that I had radiation and chemo on the same day, my mother would come and stay all day at my house until my husband came home from work and took over. It would have been nearly impossible for me to deal with the nausea and diarrhea and three kids all at once.

I was *very* lucky. In more ways than one! Sitting in that chemo treatment room, I realized that it could have been much worse. My cancer was found early, Stage 1. I only had chemo once every two weeks—IV, push, not drip. My family and friends were wonderful! And, as far as I'm concerned, I have the best doctors in the world.

My daughter is now eleven and in a new middle school, my son is now six and in the first grade, and the little one—a boy—is two. When I look back on those days I wonder how I did it. But I'm happy, healthy, and living proof that it *can* be done.

Jane Teves
Baltimore, Maryland

Marlyn Pleiman spent a number of years shuttling between Akron, Ohio, and Sao Paulo, Brazil. She wrote this letter from Brazil to two close friends, just days after her diagnosis of breast cancer was confirmed.

November 21

*H*i Cam & Judy,

Well, shit, I got breast cancer. If it's *only* that, no sweat. I am, after all, in the land of plastic surgeons and can finally get a pair of little boobs, one fake, one real. The kicker is that I just got the CAT scan tests (here you are your own medical library . . . they do treat you as if you have some say about your own body) and there's something sitting on my liver. Knowledge like that starts the butterflies in the stomach, and you can't sit still. I was very brave and jaunty about the boobs . . . I mean, it's an easy surgery and easy repair and high success rate and the treatment can be endured.

But, since I read the CAT scan . . . have not talked to the doctors yet . . . later today . . . nor shared this with anyone . . . the possibility of all those hospital horrors is a bit too close for fun. It makes the inquisition sound like a kindergarten picnic. I know the tenacity for life is so strong that people go through all that stuff voluntarily. I've seen it, and I've read their stories. I just can't believe it.

So what will I do if I have to face those horrors? I suppose the same as the millions of others who go through it daily, but God help me, please give me a little bit of grace. You should see these people I am passing in these "cancer corridors" . . . gray (okay, so I probably can't help that), hangdog face, and moans of "why me?" (why not?) No smiles, no jokes. At least don't let me take myself so seriously nor let me think I am so special that this could never occur in my life nor not be able to find the ample humor that exists in this land of tubes, chemicals, and our own version of nuclear warfare.

Speaking of which, I must leave here in another fifteen minutes to go get the bone scan.

11/30/91

The liver spot turned out to be a small cyst!

It's a nonaggressive, small tumor, already excised, but I'll go in next Tuesday for the rest of the surgery. The only other thing they found was arthritis in my hands (not exactly new news) and a variety of tiny calcifications scattered thither and yon.

I'm lucky for a number of reasons. I started this letter at the worst time, of course . . . when I read about the liver cyst and before I talked to the doctors, and I probably would not have sent this letter except that you're old friends, and this

83

is one of those biggies in life—up there with marriage and death. You remember the crazy fortune teller we went to that time? He called this within six days. He has not missed a life-changing event yet and one comforting thought . . . his dates continued until 2016!! Smile.

You guys should get the Boston Women's Health Book called, *Ourselves, Growing Older*. Mine is dated 1987, and there may be an updated version out now. I got mine as a Christmas gift about that time and did not appreciate it at all! However, it was my source for research and tackling the medical profession here and the decision to undergo treatment here and not go to the States. It really is good. It probably saved me from traditional treatment or at least from being rushed into something. And it covers everything . . . face it, chickies, we're getting up there. Heh! Heh!

Well, I will have quite a story to tell you next summer and new boobies to show you. Why not . . . half of Sao Paulo has poked and prodded them so far. It's getting so that I whip up my blouse at the least hint of curiosity on the part of anyone dressed in white.

I would stay and talk longer, but now I have to begin my fight with the insurance company. Wish me luck!

Marlyn

This letter was written one month after her surgery.

" *M*y Friends,
     So many of you have asked me so many detailed questions that, from now on, I'm just going to enclose this with my letters. It's sure to contain more than you really wanted to know."

Marlyn's Treatise on Breast Cancer.

First of all, DO NOT, repeat, DO NOT ignore a breast lump. By the time you find one, you have probably had it and the cancer from three to ten to even fifteen years. This may seem like early detection is thus null and void, but it's not. Cancer cells grow exponentially (2 cells become 4, become 8, become 16, etc.). It may take years for it to reach noticeable size; and then, doubling every growth cycle, it appears to grow much faster than before. So, as soon as you do find it and get treatment, the better off you are. How do you find it? Well, check! Every day in the shower. Don't be so squeamish.

I found mine the early part of October. I would always give a breast lump a month before seeing the doctor because I am prone to cysts, and a cyst will often disappear during a woman's monthly cycle. Then I would see if a doctor could aspirate it. (Take a needle and draw out fluid, because cysts are fluid-filled.) (No, it doesn't hurt. Honest.) Failing all that, I'd get a biopsy and insist upon *only* a biopsy, done with a local. That used to upset the surgeon, but now some doctors even recommend it. Then, after the biopsy, if it is positive, you have up to six weeks to decide the next steps.

If your doctor tells you it has to be one step, biopsy and then mastectomy if cancerous, go get another opinion. I am adamantly against one step. You need that extra time to adjust to the idea of having cancer, then educate yourself as to your options, and making *your* decision as to what type of surgery.

If your doctor is older, he may insist that you have to go right back in immediately and get surgery. Not so. You have, after all, just removed the tumor factory, so your body is much better able to handle renegade cells than it was before the biopsy, when it had to fight the tumor also. The extra time lets you find the right surgeon, the right surgery, and time to speak to women who have been there. There is no survival rate difference between lumpectomies (just part of the breast) and mastectomies. I simply chose the mastectomy because I never have gotten along well with that particular boob. I mean, three biopsies and numerous cysts? C'mon, it was outta there! I knew I had found my oncologist when the first words out of his mouth were, "Well, first of all, you have time." Then, the surgeon, when I heard he could do the reconstruction at the same time as the mastectomy. Unfortunately, I didn't wait to hear exactly what reconstruction consisted of! That had to be my denial state because I went into surgery willfully, blissfully unaware. I latched onto the idea of immediate reconstruction like a tick to a dog. It was that important to me, and, evidently, I wasn't going to muddy the waters with conflicting facts!

I found the tumor (lower front of left breast) (1/2″ x 1″) the first part of October, had the biopsy done the middle of November, and went in for the big surgery the 2nd of December. I had just had a mammogram in June that did not show the tumor, so don't depend upon those to pick up everything. Also, two mistakes were made with my first surgeon. He did not do a mammogram just before surgery to serve as a benchmark for future treatment. And, secondly, he did not order estrogen receptor tests on the tumor tissue. We got them later from the frozen block, but that is not as reliable or as thorough, and the information gained is needed for decisions on the type of adjuvant treatment. *Those are two important things!* My present doctors still haven't stopped bitching about the lack of these.

After the results came in from the biopsy, the first doctor wanted to see me that same day and wanted to schedule a mastectomy the following day. He described a zipper scar from shoulder to sternum and said we would immediately begin radiation and chemotherapy. Whoa! I let him schedule the mastectomy for a week later (which I canceled the night before) and rushed home to my handy, dandy

Boston Women's Health Book called *Ourselves, Growing Older*. If you're not older, get *Our Bodies, Ourselves*. The higher up I got in the medical profession, the closer they agreed with what I found in this book. Buy it. Then I called my doctors in the States, my friends, Strang Cancer Prevention Center in New York, and everyone else I could think of who could give me information. I did not call any family! Smile.

I found super doctors—an oncologist and a surgeon. The oncologist and I decided what to do. He ordered the usual battery of tests to make sure the tumor was a primary one. That was partly done on the basis of my tumor pathology report, but it also made a lot more sense to me. I know of several cases where the tests (bone scan, blood workup, chest X ray, abdominal CAT scan, CA-15-3 [used for future reference] Chem 24, CEA, and a couple of others!) were done *after* the mastectomy. It does a lot for your peace of mind to know as quickly as possible exactly what you are dealing with. For instance, my type of tumor is rarely encountered in breasts, so, for a few days, we seriously pondered the possibility of its being a secondary one. Then, the abdominal CAT scan detected a nodule on the liver. Well, that was the scariest time . . . but the ultrasound proved it to be a cyst. However, should events have turned out that the cancer had already spread, the surgery plans would have been completely different. Get data. If there's one thing I have learned from all this, it is that we must take responsibility for our own health strategies.

Then, as you remember, the first surgeon had planned,

with insufficient information to begin radiation and chemo treatment. First of all, if you have a mastectomy, why do you need radiation? Radiation is used with lumpectomies to prevent a cancerous lump from growing back in the same breast. If the breast is gone, you do not need radiation. Secondly, there is also hormonal therapy to consider, and many factors that go into deciding between chemotherapy and hormone therapy. While statistics show that the effects of either continue to show good results, even beyond ten years, nonetheless, neither should be ordered without good cause. Keep involved and informed during this stage. Also, my doctors did not start any supplemental treatment until after surgery was healed. This might not be possible with an aggressive, spreading cancer, but at least let the wound stop draining. (Walking around with those drainage bottles hanging out of you is really disgusting. I tried hiding mine in purses, bags, belts . . . all to no real avail. I once went walking out of the hospital lobby, dragging one, bumping along on the floor behind me. And every time you moved from one place to another, there you were, gathering up all your little pets. It was a red-letter day when I got rid of the last of them, let me tell you.)

Anyway, the treatment I am on is hormonal . . . Tamoxifen. I haven't been on it long enough to appreciate the side effects, which sound just like menopause. Here is another area where I disagree with the doctors. They shrug off these effects, such as hot flashes and dry vagina, with a wave of their hands. Well, honey, if *they* had hot flashes and withering testicles, I'd bet *they'd* be concerned! However, since my alternative is chemotherapy, and both doctors were so obviously overjoyed that they didn't have to recommend chemo, perhaps I'd better count my blessings.

BRAZILIAN DOCTORS. Many of you have asked about the doctors here. Can they speak English? Are they proficient? etc., etc. Well, being in a city of nearly 20 million people, I could find English-speaking Brazilians, who combined proficiency with that famous Latin lovableness. The surgeon's reputation here is excellent. The only thing is that I was not able to convince him (or any other doctor, except the oncologist, who wavered a bit) to leave the lymph nodes. They still think that they have to take virtually all of them. I disagree.

Anyway, Dr. Joan Carlos studied at the U.S. cancer center in Buffalo, NY; and, while he has that surgeon's arrogance, Brazilians wear it well. He listens to my arguments and is gentle about disagreeing. Brazilians have taken TLC to an art. They are careful and concerned not to hurt you; and, if they must, you feel it hurts them more. Truthfully, they fuss all over you, always call you by name, *never* rush you, and are just, well, Brazilian.

My oncologist, Dr. Rene, also has studied in the States and travels there yearly for conferences. He is my best barometer of how I am doing. It is from his looks of relaxed relief that I know I am not one of the ones giving him those lines of worry in his face.

I have learned that 150,000 women in the States were diagnosed with breast cancer in 1990 . . . nearly one in nine.

It is estimated that more than 1.5 million women will be diagnosed during the next decade. That's just in the States. That's the Cleveland Stadium filled 1800 times!!! I am lucky. My tumor was a rare, nicely nonaggressive one, which statistically shows an only ten percent recurrence rate. With therapy, that drops to less than seven percent.

THE RECONSTRUCTION. In my opinion, the pap the feminists and antisilicon implant activists are spouting is far off-base. You *are not* abnormal to not want to have a breast removed, and it is *not* totally the fault of the media and the beautiful body cult that makes us feel this way. Women are simply supposed to have two bumps on their chests. We're made that way. It's sad to give one of those bumps up. Granted, when the choice is life or death, one does what one has to do, but don't tell us not to grieve or that we feel thusly because of outside influences. I have run into women down here who are having reconstruction done *thirteen* years (!) after original surgery. It never stops bothering them. It seems to me that, with less than 1% of the implants causing trouble, and one of it fatal, they should leave it up to the women to decide whether they want them or not. You don't see them taking cigarettes off the market, and we *know* they can be fatal!

And, speaking for myself, killer of an operation that it was, I am so glad I had it done. I have no explanation for my ignorance. This was a highly specialized surgeon, highly respected for his skill in breast reconstruction. Did I think all that talent was needed for the "bumpy skin graft" I envisioned? Smile. I dug into everything else with a fine-tooth comb, but I never got the details of what they were going to do to me!

It should have been apparent in the operating room. I was cartographed with magic markers from chin to thigh. Then photographed! (I said I wanted the negatives.) I mean, this was serious. They used calipers and rulers! Also, there were three surgeons, two nurses, and an anesthesiologist. No wonder this was costing the price of a luxury car. Another clue was the head-shaking and mutters of, "This is going to be tight." (After I woke up and was inspected by self-same doctors, there was more head-shaking and comments like, "Boy, that sure is tight! Heh! Heh!" "Boy, you won't be moving for a while, heh, heh!") It turns out this particular type of reconstruction is not recommended for skinny women, and I was just on the borderline. Another woman, thinner than I, had the same surgery, and Dr. Joan Carlos said he was "scraping her backbone, hunting for fat." She said she could tell!

It's called the rectus abdominus flap. The long flat abdominal muscle (Dr. J.C. uses two muscles) is tunneled under the skin from the lower abdomen to the chest, pulled up backwards. Then it and abdominal fat is mounded up to form the breast, providing a blood supply and using as much of the original skin as possible. The rest is grafted from the tummy. The mastectomy and all the reconstruction is done through an inverted T cut at the bottom of the breast, so there are no scars at the neckline. There is a hipbone-to-hipbone cut across the abdomen, and what's left (!) of that skin is pulled down and stitched. The belly button is reset back in its proper position. (I figure mine must have been resting on my pubic bone from what I can tell.) They can also do reconstruction with muscle and fat from the back (not recommended due to scarring and requires implants as well) or from the buttocks. It's amazing.

Between the muscle yanked up and the skin pulled down, when I finally could move it was a bent-knee, hunched-shoulder, curved-back, crablike shuffle. Tom and Tess would trail behind me in public in the same fashion, making it look genetic. I did not get any unnecessary sympathy in this house.

I go back in for what they term as "details" as soon as the pulled-up muscle atrophies a bit more. But, they assure me, that is only an "overnighter" and, therefore, nothing. I was a week in the hospital with the first surgery, and it was six weeks until I was walking straight again. (I doubted I ever would!) In this second one, they cut the bent-over muscle just under the breast (but leave the artery) to finish defining the form. They make a new nipple and areola (I'm discovering that IBM's spelling dictionary was not designed for this subject), using a skin graft from the inner thigh and vaginal lips. (Yeah, I'm really looking forward to that. I've already told them to leave the good stuff.) Then, finally, they perk up the other boob to match the new one by reducing it in size and giving it a sort of facelift.

EMOTIONS. The last questions were about emotions. Shock was the word used most often in letters. No one really ever expects to get cancer, even me, who knew I was in about the ninety-eighth percentile probability. I went through all the standard phases of denial, anger, grief, and acceptance, knew that I was and where I was, but having to deal with the emotions just the same. The Boston Ladies mention that breast cancer evokes very powerful emotions in women, and that must be an understatement. I have never been so deep down furious in my life, followed by such an overwhelming sadness. It was as hard emotionally on Tom as on myself, perhaps even more so. I, at least, was not scared, and I attribute a lot of that to the prayers. There was a real sense of safety or protectedness throughout the whole experience . . . like you are safely wrapped in a cocoon, shooting the rapids . . . I felt safe but with no control over the situation at all. And just as they say, afterwards you have a heightened awareness of how sweet life is and how important relationships, family, and friends are. So, thank you, everyone, for your caring concern and prayers; but if you have any more questions, forget it!

Yours,
Marlyn

For the past ten years I considered myself a breast cancer "survivor," *not* a "victim." What bothered me the most at first was the pitying glances, and the condescending pats on the back, along with everyone's assurance that I was doing "just fine." And the fact that *every* conversation included the state of my health.

The ordeal taught me a whole new way to act around ill, old, or disabled people. Above all, let them retain their dignity. Show love and compassion but never pity.

I'm eighty now, and I don't want it now anymore than I wanted it then.

Sincerely,
Elsie M.
Indianapolis, Indiana

I am a fifty-eight-year-old woman, mother of three grown children, at present living in New York City with my husband. In May this year I was diagnosed with breast cancer and that has marked the turning point of the rest of my life.

Here's how it started: I was three months overdue for my annual mammogram. Normally I am scrupulous about getting these checkups on schedule, feeling uneasy if I go even one month over the due time, but I was unusually busy. We had houseguests and then were going to take a business trip, my husband's last since he was taking early retirement. We were eager to begin the next phase of our life together. I wasn't unduly concerned about delaying my checkup because year after year I had done so well. In fact, I prided myself on my fitness, good health, and positive attitude.

I found the lump while doing a breast self-examination. It was so large it felt almost like a normal, integral part of my breast. I wasn't sure, though, so I scheduled an exam for the next day. I told no one, not even my husband, hoping there would be nothing to tell. The young technician doing the mammogram was reassuring when I reported mild pain in my breast, dismissing it as common and usually meaningless. She took the X ray and said that she would be back only in the unlikely event of a close-up being needed. Something told me she would be back. She was. I felt raw fear.

The radiologist did a sonogram to check if the tumor was solid or a fluid-filled cyst. As I lay there on the table, I looked up at the ceiling and concentrated all my thoughts, willing the tumor to be harmless but somehow knowing it was not. Not only was the tumor solid—there was another equally large one next to it. The radiologist loomed large over my body as I lay there terrified. The center of my being was falling away. The bottom dropped from my life.

The next morning my husband and I drove to Vermont for our daughter's graduation, making stops along the drive north to set up appointments with surgeons for our return after the weekend. We had decided to tell no one the news yet, choosing instead to allow our daughter, family, and friends to enjoy the celebration rather than bringing them all down to earth with such distressing news. There would be time for that.

Vermont was never more beautiful. The campus in Burlington had that late May look of green, fresh and blossoming like our daughter's young life. I may never be back again, I told myself. Perhaps from this time on I will be experiencing one thing after another for the last time.

By midweek we had to make the dreaded phone calls, starting with our son and daughters. We tried to be matter-of-fact and optimistic for them as we simultaneously were beginning the long series of rounds of medical appointments.

In June I had a modified radical mastectomy. Twenty-three lymph nodes were found to be positive for cancer, placing me in Stage III of the disease. In July of this year I began a course of chemotherapy, which I tolerated well. This toleration factor, combined with my high-risk status, made me eligible for peripheral blood stem cell transplantation, which would enable me to take a massive dose of high-level chemotherapy in the hope of eradicating whatever cancer cells might be remaining. At first I was alarmed at the prospect, which is not without risks and also includes a long, uncomfortable hospitalization. Then, after researching the procedure, talking to others who have gone through it and are all right now, and being told by other oncologists that without it chances for recurrence of the disease are high, I made the decision "to boldly go." I wanted to be done with this business once and for all, to put it behind me and get on with my life.

This week, during a course of pre-admission tests for this procedure, a CAT scan has indicated a recurrence in the same breast. This is just two weeks from the date of the last of my chemotherapy treatments, two weeks of all kinds of physically debilitating side effects, the most frustrating being a deep, all-pervasive exhaustion the likes of which I have never before experienced. It makes this latest blow all the harder to absorb.

All my life I have been independent. I'm one who feels more comfortable doing for someone else than the reverse. Now I feel weak and vulnerable—and mortal. I need my husband in a way I never before have. I have moved from a state of interdependence to total dependence upon him. I need my family, my friends, and my medical team. I am no longer the rugged, independent individual I had perceived myself to be. The Gods, I fear, are punishing my unintentional hubris.

I have never been sure of what I believe, spiritually, and have been on a lifelong search for meaning. I am now beginning to feel closer to a sense of some force in the Universe that is aware that I am here and cares for me. I do not yet feel enough reassurance, but I am hopeful. Occasionally, to my great surprise, I find myself in tears. It can happen at any time—while talking with my husband, while looking at a child, just before a treatment. It happens quickly, before the "brave little soldier" takes over. I allow the tears now. They seem fitting.

I have created my own healing visualization: as I walk along the oceanside, I perceive the waves as the power of the Universe coming to me; the sun's rays are God's approval of the Universe and my place in it; dolphins are the joys in my life; abandoned sand castles are cancer cells in my body and will be flattened into insignificance by the power of the ocean's waves.

I perceive myself as a survivor, a fierce Amazon warrior who has already won two major battles in this war—the surgery and the chemotherapy. After each battle I retreat, recover, and then ready myself for the next. The next battle looms large right now, but I feel certain I will win that one, too. And the next, should that become necessary. I will fight as long as my own power will allow, and then some, accepting my limits only when I must. I love my life and hunger for as much more of it as I can grasp.

Yours,
Marion Hughes
New York, New York

"I want the younger generation to know that you don't have to be over thirty to get breast cancer, and it doesn't have to run in your family. I think it's important that we not stereotype this disease by age. Like my doctor said, 'Michelle, it was just plain bad luck.' "

*M*y name is Michelle Campbell. I am twenty-seven years old, married, and have two beautiful children, ages eight and four. My breast cancer was detected in September. In October I had my left breast removed. Since then I have received four months of chemotherapy, a bone marrow transplant at Duke University, and seven weeks of radiation. My treatment ended in July 1993, and so far I am disease free.

During my fight with cancer I had so much support from family and friends. My co-workers contributed over $3,000 to help pay for my trips back and forth to Duke University. People I didn't even know sent me cards and prayers. While I was receiving chemotherapy and my bone marrow transplant, I had two wonderful baby-sitters who kept my children extra hours and overnight for nothing. My mother-in-law stayed with me in the hospital during high-dose chemo, did my laundry, cooked, cleaned, and was patient.

Everyone was so helpful. But, through it all, my children and my husband were the ones who kept me going.

For them, I'd do the impossible.

Michelle Campbell
Gahanna, Ohio

$\mathcal{M}$y story begins in December 1989. I found a cancerous lump in my right breast and had a mastectomy in the spring of 1990. After I began chemo and went back to work it seemed as if everyone I met had a sister, brother, father, or some friend or family member facing cancer. Because I had been treated for it, they all expected me to have some magical words or advice. Well, there are no magical words, and I was very reluctant to share my very personal experience. How would they ever even begin to understand? But then, when my chemo was over, a dear friend asked me to put down on paper some things that helped me through the ordeal. It was for her sister. This is the letter I sent to her and, subsequently, to many others.

Don't be distressed when you have your first visit with the oncologist. On that visit he will tell you absolutely all the "bad" things that can possibly happen when you take chemo. There is only one good reason to go through this—to rid yourself of cancer cells.

Don't' worry, there are ways to handle most of the side effects. Be sure you always tell your oncologist or his nurse about the ones you are experiencing. They've heard them all and have come up with some good ways to deal with them.

You can and probably will get nauseated, although some

women don't. The doctor can prescribe medications to keep this to a minimum. If you have a tendency to get sick to your stomach, tell the doctor up front and he can give you a prescription from the beginning.

Your taste for food will change. I found that fresh fruit, boiled or baked potatoes, pasta, bread, turkey, or baked chicken were almost always tolerable. I also lived on cold cereals like Cheerios or the like. Don't buy things in great quantity, as your taste will likely change from treatment to treatment.

Drink a lot of water and other fluids. I would go from grapefruit juice to Coke to 7-UP to seltzer water or whatever I wanted at the time. I was a real coffee drinker but switched to tea while on chemo. There's always something that will taste good; you just have to keep trying until you find it. It's a lot like being pregnant and seeing what you really have a taste for, but remember to drink lots of water to flush the chemicals out.

You may lose your hair—again, some women don't. I did. It is recommended that you go the first week of your treatment and make arrangements to get a wig to have ready when you need it. By going when you still have a full head of hair you can get a wig that more closely matches your own. Your oncologist's nurse can probably direct you to a couple of places that deal with chemo patients—mine did. One advantage: You won't have to shave your legs . . .

You may get a chemical or metallic taste in your mouth—I never did. If you do, use plastic forks instead of the usual stainless steel. And keep lemon drops or peppermint hard candies to refresh your mouth.

You may lose some strength and need more rest—so be good

to yourself. Get a little extra sleep at night and let the house work go—it will be there when you're feeling better. Try to take short-cuts and prepare foods, then do your necessary jobs when you are between treatments to make the time that you are on treatment less stressful.

If you work, it's good to go back to work as soon as the doctor will let you. It distracts you from thinking so much about yourself. I found I became very self-centered and pampered myself.

I kept a type of diary—just jotted down my feeling from day to day. It helps to get your thoughts sorted out and once you know why you are feeling the way you are, you can get on with your day.

I don't know if you are religious, but my faith in God sustained me. I feel we have a chance to become closer to God. One of the up sides to having cancer is that we place a different priority on our lives and the lives of those around us. Life becomes more beautiful and we do "stop and smell the roses."

The period of time you are on chemotherapy seems to go on forever—but like every other day in your life, it has the same amount of hours.

As you can see, there are no secrets or words of wisdom to offer, just some common sense ways to get around the discomfort. It's really not the words or the advice; it's the "She's come through it, she knows," and the, "If she can do it, so can I," kind of determined attitude that will help.

I have to add this: I cannot stress enough the importance of self-examination. Only you know your body, and it is you who ultimately has the say over whether certain tests will be made. Stay alert for any changes and discuss these with your doctor. Keep yourself as educated as you can. Who knows, you may just save your own life.

Yours sincerely,
Gina S.
Coral Stream, Illinois

The seven-month period from 9/17/74 to 5/13/75 was the most awful time of my entire life! On September 17, I found a lump in my breast, the doctors informed me that my husband was dying of lung cancer, and I went home to find our house had been burglarized. My husband died December 2nd, and finally, in March, I forced myself to have a biopsy on the lump.

Even though when they put me to sleep to do the biopsy, the doctors were fairly certain the lump was not malignant, I woke up to be told that it was, and that my entire breast had been removed. Eighteen years ago, doctors didn't even think about a lumpectomy. How times have changed!

I was told to have chemotherapy even though there was no spread to the lymph nodes. I had nine months of chemo. My answer to the nausea connected was not to eat anything the day before so there wouldn't be anything in my stomach to come up. Part of the time that worked, and part of the time it didn't. I also fought a losing battle to keep my hair.

Here I was, not yet fifty, no husband, no children, horribly misshapen (or so I thought). Back then, the incision was made from top to bottom—not right to left, as is done now—so I had a bad scar from just below my collarbone almost to my waist. But I had a supportive family, a lot of friends, and a minister who drilled into my brain that life was not over for me. My doctor also kept asking me this: If a person had to lose a part of her body, wasn't it better to lose a breast than an arm, a leg, or an eye, or some part one couldn't live without? He was right, of course, but in the early months it wasn't easy.

Then, in October, I happened to run into a man whose wife had died from breast cancer. He was a former teacher of mine whom I had seen only once in thirty-five years. He invited me to lunch. Then we went to dinner, to the movies, etc. After a few weeks I could see that this was getting to be a serious relationship, so I felt I had to tell him about my surgery. He took it very matter-of-factly and, within a short time, asked me to marry him. Which I did, on April 14, 1976. Along with a new husband, I gained a daughter, son, daughter-in-law, and, since then, a son-in-law and two granddaughters.

I have to say, the last seventeen years have been the best of my life. I am truly a survivor!!

Most sincerely,
Marilyn M.
Lockport, New York

My philosophy on life, on people, on society, on suffering all changed as a result of a six-letter word that takes a mere second to say—CANCER. In 1982, at age forty, I was diagnosed with intraductal breast carcinoma. My life took on a new perspective. I cried, grieved, and wondered—why me? But I chose not to look back. I had to live in the present and make it so beautiful that it would be worth recalling.

Today is the time to express myself. Life is too short. Every day is a day of opportunity; every morning is a morning of a fresh beginning; every moment is a moment made new. I know what I put out will come back to me. Being in touch with illness does not make me wonderful. Being in touch with people who I can love, support, and share with—that makes me wonderful.

I now shake hands with the world. There is meaning to life's struggles. It is an opportunity to search deeply and find the true essence of love and life.

We need challenges to be able to see the rainbows.

Geraldine Wiess
Batavia, New York

Marjie T. lives in Concord, Massachusetts. Soon after she was diagnosed with breast cancer, she wrote this letter to "my very close friend who currently lives in California."

*M*y Dearest Friend,
You asked for a family photograph as it's been so long since we've seen each other. I was surprised that it's the same me looking out of the picture. I've changed in so many ways since I was diagnosed with breast cancer, it's hard to believe that it's not there lighting up my face for the whole world to see.

The diagnosis itself was transforming. It forced me to take an excruciatingly honest look at my life. It was kind of like rolling away a huge stone and peering at the raw earth beneath—not much there but for loneliness and despair. Somewhere along the way, joy and wonder had been erased.

Once upon a time, long ago, it was different. It was the time of youth when I dared to jump out of airplanes and tour the world on my own. It was still there as a young adult when you and I bore our lifelong friendship under a rainbow and twirled babies beneath the sky. In the era of the flower child, that was me, spontaneously grasping the glow of the moment. Once, long ago . . .

That such an insidious disease had been able to take hold under "my stone" was really not much of a surprise. A shock, indeed. A surprise, not at all. A kick off the rock, I guess! Somewhere, between the monstrous death sentence and the surgical healing statements, I remembered that bygone era of outrageousness. Gingerly, I thought I might again test the winds of life. And my journey began anew. The first breezes brought the scent of faith, all was okay. As the warming zephyrs tickled me with the notion of purpose, my sail unfurled and I was on my way. Where? I did not know.

In order to hold on to my now precious life, I did know I had to make transforming changes. So I read a lot and set about reconnecting with my spirit. As I learned to honor my inner wisdom, doors opened. People and wise ideas came in. On a leap of faith, I founded an organization to help people implement alternative ways to treat cancer. This adds meaning and fulfillment to my life. I love the work I do.

If this were to be my last day on earth, how would I want to live it? It's a question that comes up as I step into each new day. As I confront and make peace with my mortality, accepting that I will not be on this planet forever, each moment has meaning. It occurs to me that it is not so much what I do, as how I do it. I believe I have found the meaning of my life.

Have I told you lately *"I love you"*? I do.

With Love and Life's Best Blessings,
Marjie

I am one of three sisters—all of whom have had breast cancer. My youngest sister died at the age of fifty in 1972. My oldest sister has only the right side involved.

My bilateral mastectomies were done in July and September 1989. I opted not to have breast implants, not because I was seventy years old, but because I did not want to have more surgeries. My husband's first consoling words when I was told of the need for surgery were, "Now you'll look like those *Vogue* models." (We've been married fifty years.)

I resolved that when I was healed, I would contact seventy ladies (one for each year of my life) and urge them to get mammograms. I told them that I would not "bug" them, though. It would be up to them to follow through. As for me, I feel great, exercise often, and, considering the alternative, life is good.

Sincerely yours,
Esther K.
Gary, Indiana

$\mathcal{M}$y experience with breast cancer taught me to be a strong advocate for myself, to question doctors, challenge their answers, demand respect, and insist that they listen to me. This was an arduous process, and when my doctor failed to respond to me in the way I needed, I changed doctors—not an easy task when you are at your most vulnerable.

At age forty-four, when I discovered an immovable lump the size of a marble in my left breast, I went to my family doctor, who examined me. He said it was fibrocystic breast disease. He knew my family history of breast cancer. He ordered a mammogram, which came back negative (it turns out it was a false negative). He asked that I have a follow-up mammogram in three months, which was also false negative. Again, he reassured me that everything was okay.

I believe that mammograms for women under fifty with dense breasts are practically useless. The American College of Physicians and the American College of Radiologists have declined to recommend routine mammography screening for women ages forty to forty-nine. They recommend Breast Self-Exam and a yearly exam by a doctor. Mammograms should be combined with a physical exam and a biopsy to rule out the possibility of cancer when there is a suspicious lump present. My doctor failed to do a needle biopsy or refer me to another doctor. But he was the doctor, and I trusted him.

Nine months later, I was still very worried about the lump, and it seemed to be growing. I called his office for a referral to a breast surgeon.

I was diagnosed with advanced (stage IIIb) breast cancer, which had also spread to my lymph nodes. I was betrayed by the medical profession and by my own body—a double whammy. I was in shock and terrified of dying. I had a modified radical mastectomy, followed by six months of chemotherapy. For a year I experienced one assault on my body after another. My doctors did not prepare me for the pain of having my breast amputated, the length of rehabilitation, the side effects of chemo, and the fact that I would be plunged into menopause overnight. Within the space of a few months I experienced the loss of my breast, my fertility, and my estrogen.

My first line of coping was to read everything I could on breast cancer. Knowledge helps to empower you and to lessen the loss of control you experience when health-care workers take over your body.

My second line of defense was to get help wherever I could. I found a psychotherapist who specialized in treating adults with life-threatening disease. She helped me to relax, to learn to meditate while receiving my chemo infusions, and, most of all, to do nice things for myself. In weekly sessions, she made me set goals for the week: one physical, one work-related, and one just for fun. Although this sounds easy, it's a lot of work, particularly when you are nauseated all the time, bald, and depressed.

My third line of support was my wonderful husband of eight years. At my lowest points, he was always there. He took care of me, allowed me to rage, allowed me to be a "baby," and allowed me to express all my feelings. At the end of my chemo regimen, I was so weak I could hardly move, and so desperately sick and tired of living, he would "tuck" me in bed at night and kneel beside the bed while tears streamed down my face and onto the pillow. He never let me give up. I will never forget his compassion and tenderness.

Friends and co-workers told me how brave I was, but what choice do you have? Where matters of life are concerned, you do what you have to do. . . .

Sincerely,
Laura T.
Vinton, Virginia

"If you find a lump, run—do not walk—to a doctor who specializes in breast surgery and insist that the lump be removed. Whatever it is, it does not belong there. Do not believe a doctor who says it is nothing just because it is what you want to hear."
Susan Schrof is a secretary in New York City.

*I*n October of 1990, at the age of forty-two, I discovered a lump in my left breast. Prior to that I had always had regular checkups and mammograms. I immediately went to my gynecologist, who examined me and said it was probably just a cyst and nothing to worry about. He told me to stay away from caffeine, watch it for a while, and it would probably disappear. At no time did he aspirate the "cyst." As a precaution, he sent me for another mammogram, which came back negative. After six months of watching there was no change. But I decided it was time to do something. I went back to the doctor, and he then referred me to a breast surgeon.

The surgeon tried to aspirate the lump but was unable to remove any fluid. At this point, we realized we were dealing with a solid mass and not a cyst. He also felt it was nothing to worry about. However, he said the only way to be sure was to do a biopsy. On June 13, 1991, I had the biopsy done at Mt. Sinai Hospital in Manhattan. When I awoke from anesthesia the first thing I heard my doctor saying was, "We have a problem. . . ."

I could not believe what I was hearing, and all I could do was cry. My husband was at my bedside, telling me through his own tears that he didn't care what they did to me as long as I lived. The doctor said I could go home and think about it and come back in a week, or he could do the surgery—a mastectomy—the next day. I saw no point in going home to agonize over the inevitable, so I chose to stay.

I did want a second opinion, which I got from a very kind, gentle doctor, who showed up at my bedside at 10:30 p.m., held my hand while I cried, and concurred with the surgeon. He encouraged me to think about reconstructive surgery. I thought reconstructive surgery meant a tissue extender and an implant. Instead, what the plastic surgeon described was a procedure, called a TRAM flap, which uses muscle and body fat from your stomach to make a new breast.

He said if I made a decision immediately, they could do the procedure at the same time they did the mastectomy and save another hospital stay later on. Even through my tears and heartbreak, I could see the wisdom of his suggestion, and so I agreed. He telephoned my doctor immediately to arrange for a plastic surgeon to be there the next day for the surgery.

The two procedures took eight hours, but when I awoke, I still had some sort of a breast. I didn't have to endure the shock of seeing nothing where my breast used to be. Obviously, after having both abdominal and breast surgery, the recovery period was longer and more painful than if I had only had a mastectomy, but the psychological benefit was so great that I never suffered the emotional devastation which many women do. I was able to concentrate all of my energy on my physical recovery. Since the cancer had not spread to my lymph nodes, I only required six months of a mild dose of chemotherapy—just as a precaution. I have since had nipple reconstruction done as well. It has been a little over two years, and all of my checkups have been good ones.

I consider myself very fortunate that the cancer did not spread while I was following my doctor's advice to wait. If there is one message I would like to pass on to other women, it is this: **Do not wait for anything.** If you find a lump, run—do not walk—to a doctor who specializes in breast surgery and insist that the lump be removed. Whatever it is, it does not belong there. Do not rely on mammograms. *Do not believe a doctor who says it is nothing just because it is what you want to hear.* Doctors can be wrong. Make him prove it to you. Be more concerned with losing your life than with losing a breast. Life goes on without a breast; it does not go on with cancer; and the sooner you do something about it, the better your chances are of living a long, healthy life.

Sincerely,
Susan Schrof
East Rockaway, New York

You can consider me a real survivor.

In 1968 I had a radical mastectomy for cancer of the right breast, followed by chemotherapy (nitrogen mustard) and thirty-five cobalt radiation treatments. The cancer had infiltrated the blood vessels near my ribs, so the vessels were removed, and new ones were made. The lymph glands were removed from my entire right arm from chest to wrist. A few weeks later, my uterus and ovaries were removed as a prophylactic measure.

I was forty-eight years old at the time. For a year the incision drained, making it necessary to wear a dressing instead of a prosthesis. And my right arm swelled with cellulitis and lymphangitis. It still does!

I never worried about "looks" or moaned the loss of my breast. I just wanted to continue my life.

The day before surgery I planted a hedge of fifty rosebushes along the fence of my home. They are still there, and I am still here—after *twenty-five* years!

Helen H.
Chula Vista, California

Mary Andriola is a fifteen-year survivor of breast cancer. She lives in Putnam Valley, New York.

*M*y dear friends:

During the past twelve years, many women facing breast cancer have sat in my living room and shared their experiences with others in our support group. These are some of the things I've learned from these women:

Your sad times may come now and/or later. Give yourself time to cry, for it is healthy, but then move on.

Find something to enjoy each day, especially during difficult times.

An important part of the battle in fighting cancer is controlling your mind. Be media-selective. Read positive newspaper and magazine articles and watch upbeat TV shows and movies.

Watch out for statistics. If you have a 75 percent chance of staying healthy, concentrate on the positive, not on the other 25 percent.

Read Bernie Siegel's books, or try to attend one of his workshops. His beliefs will support you.

Make sure that your sense of humor is very active, for laughter is truly "the best medicine."

Take control of your health and treatment as much as you can. Listen to your body, and don't leave anything to chance. If you have unanswered questions, find another doctor or treatment plan. It will be worrisome at first, but your personal action plane will help you to cope with your breast cancer.

When worries or problems are gnawing at you, say a prayer; Peace of mind will follow.

Give yourself special treats from time to time. A little indulgence will pick up your spirits.

Look for a support group, or begin one yourself. Start small, with three or four women. Establish a rapport; then open your circle to others.

Be willing to accept help now; then be willing to be there for others later.

I wish you peace, love, and happiness.
Mary Andriola

"My twenty-seven-year-old daughter-in-law had a lump in her breast and was uneasy about going for a mammogram, so I agreed to accompany her, to lend moral support and to have my own mammogram at the same time. I figured I was doing her a favor. We went to the doctor on a Thursday. The following Sunday afternoon, the doctor telephoned each of us and instructed us to see a surgeon the following day. A needle biopsy on my daughter-in-law's lump turned out to be benign. Mine, however, turned out a little differently. . . ."

No one can say, "I know how you feel" at this time. Just like when you lose a loved one—only you can know how you feel inside. When you have seen so many people with cancer and then you're told *you* have it, all kinds of things go through your mind—at least they did mine. Everyone reacts in different ways, but let me tell you something: Those with the positive attitudes are the ones who survive the best!

When I was told there was a 60 percent chance I would have cancer again by the next year, I was determined to do everything I could to prevent it from happening. Exercise, the right foods, the right frame of mind, etc. Then, when I went for my annual checkup and they called me and said there was a problem again, that, my friend, was hard to take. But then the three masses they removed proved not to be cancer. I don't know if it was all those things I did or if I just lucked out, but I know the year went better because of my attitude.

I guess what I want to say is, you can cry a little because of what has happened to you, but don't let yourself get into a depression over it, as it's hard to pull yourself back and hard on those around you. Do what you can. Don't fight to do things you now can't do. Life is a day-to-day thing anyway, so try to enjoy each day in whatever way you can do it best. Don't forget to be positive—it's so important and, some days, probably the hardest thing to do.

Most of all, remember that all these bumps in the road only make us stronger in the long run. . . .

Love,
Betty B.
Henderson, Nevada

I was thirty-four years old when I was diagnosed with breast cancer this past April. I was shocked because I didn't think I was in a "high risk" category. My first reaction was that I wouldn't get to see my nineteen-month-old daughter grow up. To me, having cancer meant you were going to die. My fear quickly turned to anger, though, and I decided that I was going to put up a fight. I'd do whatever had to be done.

Fortunately, my diagnosis came when my cancer was still in the early stages. Not so fortunately, I had to have a mastectomy of my right breast. But I bounced back from that a lot quicker than anybody (myself included!) thought I would.

I had my last reconstructive surgery on August 3 of this year. It was hard on my body, and I seemed to be more tired than I had expected to be. I also noticed that I was gaining weight. I assumed it was from recuperating from surgery at home and eating a lot. (I never lost my appetite!)

Imagine my surprise when I found out three weeks post-op that I was pregnant! I thought my body couldn't take anything else happening to it. I was concerned about money because my medical bills were already sky-high. When I realized that I had been pregnant when I had my surgery I was afraid that I had hurt the baby, but my doctors said that nothing I had been given should have any adverse effects. Being pregnant was not going to pose any risk to me because of the kind of cancer I had (intraductal carcinoma in situ).

So, as you can see, there can literally be life after cancer. I consider myself very fortunate. Even though I will always worry a little about another occurrence, I now have something else to focus on. And I know that even if I do have another occurrence, it doesn't have to be the end of my world!!!

Jill Wise Williams
Gastonia, North Carolina

A friend gave me a pot of tulips. I planted them with a promise: If they come up in the spring, I'll be okay for another year. Throughout the winter they were covered with snow. When the snow began melting I was afraid to look. Then, one day, I saw little specks of green peeking through the dirt. Another year, I thought. Another year.
                    —From a conversation in early November 1994

*Y*ou could say that breast cancer entered my life when I was eight years old.

My mother died from it at the age of thirty in 1956, when there was little that could be done. Or at least, what was done was quite disfiguring, because of the radical Halstead method that was used then. So, for the next thirty-five years, I wondered when the other shoe would drop. In March 1991, at the age of forty-four, came those words that I had prayed would never be said to me.

I was always afraid of death. Just after my surgery I had a dream. I have never remembered a dream to this day other than this one. It is of my mother. She's in the hospital and I am a little girl and the people will not let me in to see her. She is in a room on a metal table. I am crying in my dream. Then I see her. She sits up and swings her legs over the side of the table and she says to the people, "You let her come to me." And I go in to my mother and she says to me, "Marilyn, it's going to be okay, darling."

Now, two years later, with a double mastectomy, chemotherapy, and radiation all behind me, I have a different outlook on life. There is a freedom that comes with this illness, and living through the not-so-pleasant treatments has given me a new lease on life. I squeeze as much as possible into every minute of the day, and I have become quite an advocate in the fight against breast cancer. The strength that comes from coping with this illness has helped me with everything in my life, not just one particular event.

Marilyn Farrar
Oswego, Illinois

*O*n December 23, I got an early Christmas present. Test reports after biopsy revealed I had breast cancer!

My husband and I decided not to reveal the news until after the New Year. The decision was made primarily because if it was to be my last Christmas, I wanted it to be a joyous one. (To this day, my eighty-seven-year-old mother knows nothing of my cancer.) On January 29, 1994, I had the very first surgery in my sixty-one years of life. The results, as reported to us, were exhilarating—*they got it all!* Nothing had spread. I was cured. For insurance, I received some radiation. But for all intents and purposes, I was cured!

A year later I started to feel pain in my right hip. It progressed to where I started to limp. It was recommended that I have a bone scan. Afterward, I was told I had degenerative bone disease. The advice was to walk, walk, walk. I listened to the doctors and walked until I could not take a step without help. I called an orthopedic surgeon who took X rays which clearly showed that my femur bone was cracked, eaten away by cancer that had metastasized from the breast. In May they gave me a new hip and more radiation.

They gave me three months to live, and suggested chemotherapy and a bone marrow transplant, which they said they hoped could postpone the inevitable. It was at this point that I took charge of my own destiny. I told my oncologist that I didn't need his help to die; I could do that quite well on my own. I was going to find someone to help me live.

I believe that all of us have cancer in our bodies, but most people get rid of it quite naturally. People like me, who have lost their immune system, cannot successfully fight some diseases, cancer included. At the time, I spoke with a friend, a cancer survivor who also was given three months to live—in 1987. He told me of an allergist/nutritionist who cured him.

It took several months to get an appointment. During this time my wonderful, caring daughter took a leave of absence from her job in Utah and came home to help me regain my health. She is a vegetarian and extremely knowledgeable about nutrition. We changed my diet to fresh fruits and vegetables, no packaged foods, no canned foods, no meat, no dairy, no citrus, no salt, no sugar.

My first visit with the doctor lasted three hours. I was tested for and discovered what my system was allergic to and what my system was lacking. I came away with fifty-four vitamins and minerals plus a very restricted diet.

I'm still here and I'm now referred to as "a walking miracle." If that's what people think, so be it. I prefer to think of myself as someone who took charge of her life and made the decision to go alternative medicine. I'm glad I did!

Yours,
Marjorie St. C.
Danvers, Massachusetts

"My story is the same as that of millions of women out there—the fighting of the battle, the coping with the loss of a breast, the emotional recovery after chemo is over and the doctor's appointments are spread farther and farther apart. And the fact that we now face life, and maybe death, much differently than do our family, friends, or peers."

y story begins in 1975 when my father, Al Richmond, was diagnosed with breast cancer. He had a lump next to his nipple that he thought was a mosquito bite that just wouldn't go away. We're not quite sure how long he had this before he told my mother about it. But he was immediately referred to an oncologist by his physician. From that moment on, life for us all would never be the same.

He had a radical mastectomy, cobalt treatments, and was treated at the NIH with some experimental procedures. He truly was a hero, my dad. He never complained; he never asked why. He just did what he had to do. My mom would sew pockets into his T-shirts and stuff them so he could still go to the beach and not have an "inverted" appearance. It didn't stop him from living. But he knew his days were numbered. He had heard from too many people, too many times, that it is so rare for a man to have breast cancer. It was a long, hard, two-year battle that he ultimately lost.

Then, we come to 1988. I had been going to my gynecologist regularly, especially after having two children—one in 1984 and one in 1986. I happened to mention to him that I had a "hot water running sensation through my breast" for a couple of weeks. That was the best way I could describe it. Although I was only thirty-two, he suggested that I have my first mammogram and see what that was all about.

The mammogram showed that I had calcifications, not uncommon at all in women. The doctor said if they didn't change, I'd be okay. So, we scheduled another mammogram six months later. They had not changed. I was home free for a year, and then I was to come back. Eleven months later I was inundated with cancer in the form of micro-calcifications throughout my entire breast. I had at least four second opinions, and they all said the same thing: Removal of the breast was the best route to take because having so many lumpectomies would leave me "breastless" anyway.

So, in April of 1990 I had a modified radical mastectomy with immediate reconstruction. That, too, was an ordeal, because my surgeon had never worked with a plastic surgeon in the operating room and wasn't willing to do so. After much discussion and argument he agreed to do it. To this day, four years later, my surgeon comments on what a wonderful job "they" did on my breast; and he has since worked with other plastic surgeons in doing the same. I feel very proud to have been his first.

My emotions ran the gamut back then, as they do now. Trying to make sense of it all, trying to accept it on one hand and refusing to believe it on the other. Confusion, depression, ups, downs, an indescribable tiredness that wouldn't go away. Then I would look at Bruce and my girls, Jen and Lauren, and thank God that I was alive.

After being told that I did not need chemo because my lymph nodes were clean I decided to take it anyway. It was at a time when the news was splattered all over the place with headlines of "Node-Negative Women Found to Do Better with Chemo." I decided to take that challenge. I knew what I was up against and, because I wanted more children, that was the hardest decision to come to.

It was the worst six months of my life. Not only did I have nausea all the time from the drugs, but I also had "psychoneurogenic nausea" as well. So, every time I got in the car to go to chemo or got in the elevator at the hospital or saw my chemo nurse or even saw a hospital on TV(!), I threw up. Anywhere, anytime. Still, I wouldn't have done it any differently. I feel I made the right decision at the right time in my life. I also had my implant put in right before the big headlines that said, "Silicone is no good!" But I wouldn't have done that any differently either. You do what you have to do when you have to do it. You can't look back. You are in survival mode. You are working toward one thing, and one thing only: STAYING ALIVE! And having a decent quality of life doing it. I have always felt I may not have the quantity of life that I expected to have, but, damn it, I will have the quality!

I now enjoy counseling other people with breast cancer. Although I'm only thirty-eight years old, I feel like I know more than most about this disease. I believe support groups, when people are ready for them, are valuable beyond words. It's there that you learn the techniques of survival. And it's there that you can cry, laugh, and be angry—a place where you can be honest about and to yourself. If you don't have the support of family and/or friends, you will get more than your share's worth here. And if you do have family and friends who support you, it will still do you a world of good. Trust me. I know.

Not all the changes that have happened to me are bad. Blue skies are now bluer. Flowers are more beautiful. Songs are prettier. Problems are smaller. Friendships are more important. Family is everything. From day one, my husband Bruce has been my strength. He accepted my cancer, my mastectomy, my hair loss, without blinking an eye. In the hospital he changed my dressings, fixed my drains, fed me— he was known as the "man who never left his wife's side." We've been through Hell. Together. He's never let me down.

At my support group, when introducing ourselves, Bruce said, "I'm Bruce, Amy's husband, and I'm a co-cancer patient. Amy has cancer, so I have half of it." Can you believe that? He loves me, no matter how I look or how I feel. How can I ever say I'm unlucky? I have Bruce. And no matter what, I will always feel lucky.

In a roundabout way, this all brings me back to my dad. After describing the "hot running water" sensation through my breast to many of my doctors since that time, they have all agreed on the same thing—that that had nothing to do with my illness. I have come up with the only solution to that sensation. It must have been my dad, telling me to get to a doctor because trouble was a-coming! I feel he saved my life. Did I ever think like this before? No. Did I ever believe in messages sent from beyond? No. Do I now? You betcha. I am a survivor. Just like my dad was.

Sincerely,
Amy Seich
Canton, Massachusetts

I wrote this poem when I was newly diagnosed and very, very scared.

A forever patient.
The end of life as I knew it.
The beginning of survival.
The anger. The fear. The unknown.
Life has changed. I have changed. Things are never to be the same.
Controlled crying.
Guilty feelings.
March 27th—the day the music died.
> *Afraid of dying of cancer.*
> *Afraid of living with cancer.*
My dad. My mom.
Bruce. The children.
Support from friends.
Support from strangers.
Anonymous voices offering help.

Losing my breast. Seemingly a small sacrifice.
Acceptance. Denial. Acceptance. Denial.
Chemotherapy. Baldness. Dread.
Exhaustion.

Happiness? The future?
Normalcy? Recovery?
Prognosis.

Uncertain.

$\mathcal{M}$y entire life turned around when I heard the words, "It's cancer." My first thought was that there was some mistake; the doctor couldn't be talking to *me!* And yet, the day before, in a telephone conversation with a very good friend, I said I knew my lump would be malignant. Call it intuition, perception, ESP, or whatever, I just knew the outcome would be bad news.

I had infiltrating ductal carcinoma. My tumor was 1.5 centimeters. I chose a lumpectomy with six weeks of radiation. I had some major problems, some swelling, a lot of redness and slight fatigue. But I'm most satisfied about the road I took. And I was exuberant when the treatments were over.

One of my greatest angers is to repeatedly hear about risk factors. I honestly do not believe in them. I've always taken very good care of myself. I never smoked, rarely drink, and breast cancer doesn't run in my family. (Although a year later I found out my father's mother was diagnosed with breast cancer when she was in her late seventies, she lived to be eighty-seven.) My best protection was the fact that I was a very young mother. I had two daughters at age twenty-two and had two more children, sons, by age thirty. I remember reading how protected I was and wouldn't have to worry about breast cancer. Somehow, I wanted to blame myself. It took me a year to realize that I wasn't at fault, I did nothing wrong. Breast cancer even happens to men.

Sincerely,
Gerry McGahan
Hanover Park, Illinois

This is the first time I have written about my experiences with my breast cancer and I have to admit that even after five years, it is still therapeutic to share it. My cancer was detected early by a mammogram when I was sixty years old.

I opted for a mastectomy, a fortunate decision for me because after the surgery it was discovered in pathology that there was another area of cancer in the breast that had not been detected. If I had opted for a lumpectomy, I would still have had the disease.

I had a "tram flap" reconstruction immediately following the mastectomy. Tissue for the reconstruction was taken from my abdominal area and moved up to form a new breast. I have an excellent cosmetic result. Although my new breast is numb, I need no prosthesis and I look normal, even in a swim suit. This reconstruction has made me feel "whole" again, and has been probably the single greatest contributing factor to my mental recovery. I never saw myself without one breast, and now I am so used to seeing the "different" breast that even when I step out of the shower, I sometimes need to remind myself that I had cancer.

I am now healthy (as far as I know) and happy, and do anything I would have done if I had never had breast cancer. I have traveled to many of the places I wanted dearly to see. I recently rode a Wave Runner on Lake Powell.

And at age sixty-five, I'm still tap dancing!

Sincerely
Janet Meyer
Vista, California

*O*n May 30th, 1991, my cancerous breast was removed. I breezed through everything. My surgeon came in to see me after surgery and found a woman in a pink and white pajama short set with matching earrings and makeup all done. He wondered where his patient had gone. My spirits, my attitude shocked everyone.

I came home from the hospital on June 6th and waited for this experience to change my life. I had read articles about people who, having gone through life-and-death situations or having suddenly realized their own mortality, made drastic changes in their lives. But I didn't feel different. My family and friends were hurting for me more than I was. So when, I wondered, was this new "me" going to emerge?

A month into my chemotherapy (I was already back at work) I read in the newspaper about a breast cancer support group that was offered near to where I lived. I thought I should join a group because I believed that one day I wouldn't be able to cope with the cancer or the chemo or the realization of everything that took place. So on August 26, 1991, I walked into the Cancer Institute of Brooklyn and attended my first meeting.

The group was comprised of women who had had lumpectomies, modified radicals and bilateral mastectomies.

Some never underwent surgery at all, opting for chemotherapy treatment indefinitely. There were women who were in a "wait-and-see" stage, who had what was considered a precancer stage. The ages ranged from young (early thirties) to seniors (early eighties). The group even had mother-daughter members.

We cross all ethnic lines in this group. We are white, black, Hispanic, Asian. We represent a true melting pot of society. As a group we prove that cancer does not discriminate. We have become a family. I learned something at these meetings. I realized what this group was offering to *me*—a chance to help others. Suddenly I was able to speak to women and comfort them. Show them through example that you don't always lose your hair on chemotherapy, that sickness doesn't always go hand-in-hand with chemo, that what you wear and how you dress does not have to change—you can still be attractive, sexy, and vivacious, and that you don't only glow when you are pregnant, but throughout any part of your life.

I found I was able to reassure people, advise them how and when to take their antinausea meds, tell them what foods are easiest to eat and at what temperature. Things sometimes even the best doctor forgets to tell you. People were comfortable speaking to me about their fears. Co-workers began asking me to call their sisters, their daughters, or someone with breast cancer whom they had heard about through word of mouth. I was able to refer my former mother-in-law to a surgeon when she discovered a lump in *her* breast. I discovered that by talking with women, and helping them, I had found a purpose to my own life. The change I was waiting for had started.

In a way I feel like a pioneer as far as my group and other mastectomy patients that I have come in contact with are concerned. I feel that through all the stages of my mastectomy and my recovery, I have been a source of inspiration to so many others. Because I had cancer my life has now crossed paths with many wonderful women. Women who have helped me laugh and seen me cry. Women who have touched my soul in ways I never imagined. Each woman has enriched my life with the memory of herself, and that is something I will have the rest of my life.

Love,
Marie Russo
Brooklyn, New York

Selma Larson is a retired teacher, "only a few months shy of seventy-five."

*P*ersonally, I have never considered being a breast cancer survivor a really big deal. In August of 1979 I retired from Adrian College. I had my annual physical and a mammogram, and a few days later my husband and I went off on a trip. After we arrived home my doctor called to recommend that I get a biopsy. I went to a surgeon whom I had known for many years. I knew him to be a perfectionist and I trusted him as a friend. We talked about what approach to take and decided that, if the lump proved to be malignant, it was not necessary to wake me; but he should do the modified radical mastectomy as required. Remember, this was in a small town in 1979, before much information was available on alternatives. Today, I would not bypass the opportunity to rethink the decision to have such intrusive surgery.

Life got back to normal, more or less. I was called by various departments at the college to work as a substitute. But when some of them found out I had had a bout with "cancer," they were afraid to get near me. Keep remembering, this was in 1979. Cancer was something you did not talk about very much. One day I saw an advertisement seeking people to serve on an advisory council for the regional Area Agency on Aging. One thing led to another, and I was appointed to fill an unexpired term on the Board of Directors. From there I was appointed to the Michigan Senior Advocates Council and presently chair the health-care committee. In May of 1993 I was asked to be the Senior Citizen Congressional Intern in Washington, D.C., with Senator Donald Riegle of Michigan. In addition, I now write a weekly column on aging issues for our local daily newspaper.

You ask how does this relate to breast cancer? Never in my wildest dreams would I have thought that I could have the self-confidence to do some of the things I now find so easy to accomplish. I was the typical compliant housewife and mother. After losing a gifted son in a drowning accident at age twenty-six just a couple of years before I retired, and after a bout with cancer, I figured I had nothing to lose. I was going to do whatever interested me. In the process, I have won many awards as well as the utmost respect from my family, my siblings, and my peers. I have become so strong.

I have had no indication of a recurrence of cancer during the fourteen years following my mastectomy, but I am carefully monitored. At the time of my surgery, follow-up treatment was not given, so I probably was also very lucky.

I keep so busy that I forget all about it and don't give cancer a second thought.

Sincerely,
Selma Larson
Adrian, Minnesota

In May of 1986 I realized that my right breast was very hard. At first my doctor said there wasn't anything wrong. I kept complaining, though, and he decided to do a biopsy. I was diagnosed with inflammatory carcinoma. The surgeon didn't give me much hope.

I went to Fox Chase Cancer Center in Philadelphia for the second opinion. There, I was introduced to Dr. Corey Langer, who gave me all the hope I needed. I had a five-month course of chemotherapy immediately. When that was over I had radiation for five weeks. On March 11, 1987, I had my breast removed. The result was no cancer!

It will be seven years in March that I am cancer-free. I thank God that I'm here today to be able to write about it.

Yours truly,
Peg Steinberg
Philadelphia, Pennsylvania

Am I a breast cancer survivor? I am to my mind! I have survived the initial shock of diagnosis, a mastectomy, chemotherapy, radiation, and the loss of a child.

I was thirty-three years old and four and a half months pregnant. During my first prenatal exam I had a breast exam and the lump was detected. At the time of surgery the tumor was five centimeters with positive lymph nodes. This was an aggressive cancer, and the doctors felt that delaying treatment could jeopardize my life. I have two other small children, ages three and a half and two, who needed me. A week after they took my breast, they took my baby.

Chemotherapy was difficult but not impossible. My husband took charge of the kids, and the ladies from my church took charge of feeding them. A few days after each treatment, I would begin to feel normal. Outsiders looking at me couldn't tell that I had cancer. For some reason that was important to me.

Then I lost my hair. Now, I felt like I *looked* like I had cancer. I never thought I'd miss it, and when it grows back I vow to never have another "bad hair day."

Radiation was not as difficult as chemo. But still, during my treatments I fell into a depression. I would lie there each day and concentrate on the cancer, directing the radiation "rays" to destroy the cancer cells. It was during this period that I decided to do something, anything, to help other women through this. I am now making gowns for breast cancer patients to wear during their radiation treatments. Something to make one feel prettier than those awful, hospital-issued, air-conditioned robes. It's only a small thing, but it makes me feel like I've contributed something to the cause.

I'm not certain how much of a "survivor" I am since I just finished my treatments. But I sure feel like I have survived something! I am still alive and putting my two children to bed each night. I plan to be doing that for many years to come.

With best wishes,
Cinda R.
Vancouver, Washington

Two years ago, on a Monday morning at nine, I went for my annual mammogram. By the time I got home at two, there was a message on my answering machine to call my doctor. By four-thirty that afternoon my husband and I were back at the doctor's office. He told me they had seen six dots, no larger than a pinpoint, which he called "calcifications." The six dots turned out to be cancerous. He recommended a mastectomy and suggested that I also consider the healthy breast well, since I had a 17 percent chance of recurrence in that breast. He wanted me to think about having a double mastectomy. I cried. I talked. I was in shock. But after much thought I decided to go ahead with it.

That was two years ago. My surgeon has put me on tamoxifen and checks me out every four months. Every time I think of the word "calcification" I get a chill. Most of the time it's not cancerous and they can just watch you. But as you can see, it can also turn out to be cancer. I never had a "lump" or "thickness," so actually the mammogram and my doctor's awareness saved my life.

Rosalie Leerman
Westminster, Maryland

Christine Zifchack is thirty-four. Her cancer was diagnosed when she was twenty-nine years old.

*T*here's so much I would love to say, but it seems that a lot of things are hard to put onto paper. My story isn't much different than thousands of other women's, and although my experiences and feelings are typical of so many others faced with their own mortality, they still have had some very dramatic effects on me and those close to my heart.

After the initial shock passed and decisions were made I knew I had to do whatever was needed to survive and become a positive role model. Having three daughters of my own (then ages seven and four-year-old twins), a sister, and a mother who were all now at an increased risk, I read everything I could find about this disease, and spoke with a number of survivors for additional information. All of this became a weapon for me against this fight of my life—one which I hoped, prayed, and believed I could win.

I don't want to say that I'm *glad* that I had breast cancer—none of us would ever wish for a disease—yet so much has happened to me and those I love that wouldn't have taken place otherwise. First, I quit smoking the day I went into the hospital. Second, many women I know went for their first mammogram knowing that it *can* happen to someone they care about. We've all become more aware of health and women's concerns. And most important—we've all realized how important we are to each other and how much we are loved. And we no longer hesitate to say so.

Something that I do feel, though—is that whenever any of us face any crisis, it's important to keep—or at least attempt to keep—our heads up and our sense of humor even higher! Laughter really is a very good medicine. I've learned to laugh off what I can, and joke about the rest. Cancer is very serious and very deadly, but if we dwell on all the facts we get depressed and in turn can depress our immune system. And our support system and well-meaning friends respond to us much better (after the shock!) when we are lighthearted—at least most of them do.

I had an implant at the time of surgery and got a kick out of comparing aloud my old and new boob! I'd get some weird looks from my family, although eventually we'd all laugh. My husband didn't always appreciate my "morbid" sense of humor—but I needed it in order to release my tension and fear of dying. Death could have been a possibility, and it was the only way I could communicate to him the fears I knew he had but didn't want me to know he was thinking.

Very early after my surgery I heard the statement that "90 percent of the cure comes from above the shoulders." I've never felt so strongly about anything. I know that many women die of the disease within a short period of time— but positive thinking can enhance our lives so much more regardless. Positive thinking—visual enhancement and humor—support systems—good medical care—trust in your physician will help take care of us and play out our role that God has created for us.

Some family members couldn't understand why God would let this happen to me at such an early age. Being thirty, with three young daughters—it could have seemed like a punishment. But then I feel (and felt then), "Why not me?" It happened. I'm alive, and so much of my family has benefited from it. We all became closer. I changed some destructive behavior and really learned to appreciate life, as did we all.

I can't say I'd ask for any of this to happen again—not to anyone else that I love, but having survived these last five and a half years, I'd like to think I could handle most anything. And lastly, please don't ever (anyone) complain to me about getting older! I'm so happy every year on my birthday knowing I've survived and can chalk up another one. I can't wait until I'm old and can say the words, "twenty—thirty—forty years ago—when I was diagnosed . . ." Whether any of us lives another week, or a month or twenty years, our lives are what we make them. Each and every day is a gift from God, and if I can touch the life of another person because of what has happened to me in mine—then I'll know that my life was not in vain.

Good luck and God bless,
Chris Zifchack
Girard, Ohio

$\mathcal{M}$y first experience with breast cancer came in the fall of 1973, when I was treated by a radical mastectomy for a lump I had found the year before. Why the delay in treatment? It was simply a case of being told by my physician, who had always known me as a perfectly healthy person, that it was "nothing." Fortunately for me, the surgery, though radical, was uncomplicated and skillfully done, right in our small community hospital.

If life begins at forty, this was an unexpected rebirth! It was the beginning of a productive time of self-knowledge, spiritual growth, and involvement in community activities that were important to me. On a physical level, I felt fine and quite enjoyed a period of R & R, the first since my three children were born more than a decade before. Perhaps I was also enjoying the benefits of a "scare" without the disastrous outcome that family and friends had feared or anticipated.

It would be thirteen years before a second lump appeared, suddenly, in the remaining breast, and again the biopsy report was that of breast cancer. But by this time lumpectomies were in vogue. It was 1986. There were choices I could make. One was lumpectomy, which would necessitate my receiving radiation in a medical center a difficult hour-and-a-half drive away. The other choice was to have a second mastectomy.

For me, it was a simple choice. Not being an enthusiastic long-distance driver, I opted for the mastectomy, which I knew would not be a problem. Besides, a second mastectomy would assure me that I could return to an appearance of being "even" and choose the size that I wanted to be.

Today, it's more than twenty years since that first surgery and I can say, thankfully, that my greatest health problem is not breast cancer, but rather the aches and pains of arthritis!

> Very truly yours,
> Patricia J. H.
> Peterborough, New Hampshire

$\mathcal{I}$'m a young seventy-one-year-old. Seven and a half years ago, after a shower, I looked in the mirror and noticed an inverted nipple in my left breast. Of course I was shocked. Immediately, I went to a surgeon-oncologist. The mammogram showed two lumps. After the operation and all tests—I had one positive lymph node—the doctor claimed the cancer had been in me for eight years. I felt fine in those years, like a forty-year-old. Cancer is a sneaky enemy.

The cancer was in remission for three years, but in April of '93 it erupted again. The tumor marker test CA 15-3 is normal at thirty. Mine was forty, then climbed to seventy-nine within three years. FDA claims that the test isn't too accurate. I had a bone scan that showed that the cancer had spread to my bones in the hip and spine. I immediately went to Sloane Kettering, where I was put on male hormones and steroids. In three years, though, they no longer helped. Now I'm on chemo and radiation. I'm too old for a bone transplant or stem cell.

I've been on tamoxifen, steroids, anti-hormones, chemo for seven and a half years, but I seem to be running out of treatments. All that is left for me is stronger chemo and taxol. Meanwhile, I try to keep abreast of things. I ask my doctor about all the new treatments. I call the National

Cancer Institute at 1–800–4–CANCER to keep abreast of things. I have all the material available, including alternatives.

I cannot cry, so my outlet is to go to a cancer support group where I can freely talk about my condition. I can air it out. I have holy water from Lourdes, Congysco, Jerusalem. I have a positive attitude, which I understand helps greatly. I pray, have crystals, wear my birth sign gem (amethyst), and am looking into alternative treatments should we run out of medical treatments. I even take Essiac, an herb brew I get from a nurse from Canada. I'm trying very hard to stay alive.

Your luck is the doctor you pick. They are not gods. They do their best, but you must do your own research and be in charge!

Love you for caring,
Lucrezia Victor
Syracuse, New York

$\mathcal{I}$n October of 1974 I was shocked to hear the surgeon tell me that the tumor he removed from my breast was malignant. It took twenty-four hours to learn the extent of the disease and what treatment I had a choice of. That was the longest twenty-four hours of my life. All I could think of was: was I going to live or die?

My surgeon explained that if I wanted to live and hopefully not have another occurrence, I should have a radical mastectomy. Since I had worked in the medical field almost nine years he didn't have to explain to me what this entailed. The next day I had a radical mastectomy. I was left with a scar almost the whole length of my chest area. I had been scraped clean to my rib cage. My remaining skin was so tight, you could see my heart beat.

I was told I could not return to work for three to four months. Since I was twenty-seven years old, divorced, and had a two-year-old son to support, I was determined not to let this change my lifestyle. I returned to work three weeks after my surgery and haven't stopped yet.

At the time of my surgery I had been dating someone for a year, but after the surgery he was unable to cope with my situation, so we went our separate ways.

For the first three years I very rarely dated. Then, in 1977, I went out on a blind date that a girlfriend of mine arranged.

157

After dating this man for a month I knew I was in love with him. This presented the problem of telling him about my mastectomy. To my surprise, he explained that he was in love with me and that the mastectomy did not matter to him. Talk about being on "Cloud Nine"! We were married two months later and still love each other as much as we did the first day we met.

In 1984 I made the decision to have breast reconstruction. My husband was against it, but I wanted to do it for myself. I wanted to be able to wear a bikini and a low-cut blouse again, which I can now do. It has changed my life tremendously.

I now have a business of my own, working out of my home. I have a fourteen-year-old daughter who was diagnosed as having juvenile diabetes at the age of five. I started my business in order to be able to spend more hours at home with her and to help her cope with the teenage years that are ahead. I know that I am an example to her, proving that, even though you have a disease, this doesn't mean there is no future—you can live a long life. I always encourage her not to give up.

Like most women who have gone through my experience, I live with the fear each day that the cancer may return. I have become a stronger person, though, and have learned not to take life for granted anymore.

Sincerely,
Linda J.
Brookfield, Georgia

I am a breast cancer survivor of six years, four months. I was forty when I was diagnosed. I was a wife, a mother of two (ages seventeen and eight), and an active participant in life. I had a radical mastectomy and chemotherapy. Anyone who has been through this experience has stories—good and bad—and tips for coping, physically and emotionally. I have two I'd love to share with you.

First, *be responsible for your own health*. I found a large mass in my left breast only four months after my annual mammogram. Had I relied *only* on the mammogram, I certainly would not be healthy today. Every woman needs to use good sense. See your doctor regularly and listen to his/her advice and counsel. But if you feel something isn't right, regardless of what a test or a physician has revealed, CHECK IT OUT. Have another test, get a second opinion, don't go crazy, but be responsible for your body and its care.

Second, *accept help*. As an independent woman with a husband who traveled a lot, I'd been used to doing most everything for myself. I had a part-time job at that time, a home to manage, children to care for, meals to cook, etc., as well as attending to the church and community and school activities I was involved in. As chemotherapy began to take its toll on me, I realized that I couldn't do everything. This was very hard for me. I wasn't used to depending on others, but I soon saw how much I needed the help that was being offered. I accepted meals, housecleaning, rides to treatment, rides for my kids, books, flowers, and those ever-needed hugs and handholding visits. Being given so much care by so many friends has made me a more caring person. And not only did it help me immeasurably, it helped my friends as well. My acceptance of their gifts of food, time, and love healed their broken hearts as I struggled to heal my broken body. None of us are the same today because of that time in our lives. Accept the help and then, when you are strong again, help someone else.

Sincerely,
Patty Whiten
Lake Forest, Illinois

I was recently diagnosed with malignant calcifications. I underwent a modified radical and am now undergoing chemotherapy. It might seem odd, but since I found out that I had cancer my life changed for the better. Like many women with breast cancer, I was initially filled with anger. I went through a depression, the feeling of being ugly. Eventually, though, I realized that even though I am powerless over my disease, I do have the power to control my life. In other words, I had a choice. I could mope around and feel sorry for myself, or I could accept my disease and live life to the fullest. I chose to accept my disease. Now, if there is anything or anyone in my life that is not good for my health, I detach it from my life. I have a lot of faith in God and in my medical team. This means a lot to my recovery. And I take one day at a time. Why worry about tomorrow? Today's not over yet.

Neysa Abt
Brooklyn, New York

"At first we made 'small talk' while he checked the incision. I watched him for clues of what was coming. I noticed how he was looking everywhere in the room except at me, and then came the words I'd feared. 'Kaye, it never gets easier to tell someone this . . .' "

*O*ne evening in November 1988 I was watching a TV special called "Destined to Live," in which several women and men described their experiences with breast cancer. As I watched, it occurred to me that I had been procrastinating making an appointment for my gynecological checkup. I remember thinking, "If these women and men can go through all they've been through, I can certainly go in for a checkup." I made an appointment with my doctor the very next morning.

The checkup went well and my doctor said that since I'd recently turned thirty-five, he recommended I get a baseline mammogram. He said he wasn't insisting that I go—that there was nothing unusual about my checkup—but he felt it was a good idea to follow the American Cancer Society guidelines on mammography. I agreed and made the appointment. Two days later I had the mammogram done. It was late in the morning, and as I was leaving, the technician told me she'd send a report to my doctor within the next couple of days.

Four hours later I was back at my office when my phone rang. It was my doctor calling to tell me there was something on my mammogram that was very worrisome. He wanted me to contact a breast surgeon that afternoon. In fact, he was going to call the surgeon as soon as we hung up and wanted me to call immediately to get an appointment. My first words were, "You're kidding me." He assured me he was not, and couldn't emphasize enough the urgency of seeing a surgeon. This was a Friday afternoon at 3 o'clock. In less than an hour I was on my way.

As I drove to the surgeon's office, I realized that I didn't even know whether the problem was on my left side or right side. I wracked my brain trying to remember if there were any clues that there was something wrong. There were none. I hadn't felt anything unusual, nor had I had any discomfort. In fact, I had been feeling great. My gynecologist had done a physical examination and had not found any lumps. How could there be something so alarming and I didn't even know about it?

The surgeon showed me the mammogram of my right breast. One area appeared much denser than the surrounding tissue. It appeared to have long "fingers" radiating out from its core. He wanted to do a surgical biopsy, but it was late on Friday afternoon and no operating room was available. He suggested a needle biopsy in the meantime to see if it would provide any useful information. Within half an hour we had the pathology report—the mass contained abnormal cells, but they couldn't conclusively say they were cancer cells. We would have to wait for the results of the

163

surgical biopsy to know for sure if the tumor was malignant.

I spent the longest weekend of my life, wondering what the following week would hold for me. On Monday afternoon I had a surgical biopsy, and two days later I returned to the surgeon's office to hear the results. He explained that I had a two-centimeter tumor that was malignant—infiltrating ductal carcinoma. I remember very little else about that office visit, other than that he was talking about removing part or possibly all of my breast. He told me to take a couple of days to absorb the diagnosis and then come back and he'd review my options with me again.

There were so many things to consider. I had been given the option of having a modified radical mastectomy or a lumpectomy followed by radiation treatments. I also mulled over whether to be reconstructed or not, and, if reconstructed, whether to be immediately reconstructed or wait until later. Over the next week I spent hours and hours reading everything I could get my hands on regarding breast cancer and its treatment. I went back and talked with my doctors some more to clarify what I was learning about my choices. I had never before had to learn so much so quickly in order to make such an important decision. After sorting through the options I decided that the right thing for me to do was have a mastectomy. I also decided that reconstruction was not for me.

On December 2 I had my breast removed. My prognosis was good. There was no indication that the cancer had spread beyond the site of the tumor. The doctors felt that we had found the cancer early enough so that my chances of long-term survival were quite good. I was told that follow-up should include some sort of adjuvant therapy, either chemotherapy or hormonal therapy. I chose hormonal therapy and started taking the drug tamoxifen.

I returned to work within a month of my surgery and started on the road to recovery. For eight weeks I attended support group meetings and discussed all aspects of my recovery with women who understood exactly what I was going through. As time passed and I continued to educate myself about breast cancer, I realized how lucky I had been.

This whole experience was like an awakening for me. Up until that time, I had been gliding through life on automatic pilot. It seemed like an endless ride; it didn't enter my mind that my life could be threatened at thirty-five years of age. I had attained many of my goals and was comfortable with my life. I was single, had relocated to Oregon, bought a house, had a good job, enjoyed my circle of friends. And I took it all for granted. There still was a lot more I wanted to do, though, and it didn't involve acquiring more "things." I joined the group that had helped me so much, the Breast Cancer Outreach Program at St. Vincent Hospital and Medical Center in Portland, Oregon. It allowed me to offer hope and support to other women, as it had so generously been given to me.

SECOND DIAGNOSIS

In the fall of 1991 I started experiencing problems with my left arm. I would suddenly lose mobility . . . I couldn't roll down the car window or reach out and put letters in the drive-up mailbox at the post office. The problem would persist for a day or two and then clear up. The first time I assumed I must have strained my arm while doing yardwork. The second time I couldn't recall any particularly stressful activities that would affect my arm and was becoming concerned. The third time I realized that, as crazy as it seemed, the problem with my arm flared up right before my period was going to start. That's when I became alarmed. Was there a connection somehow with my breast cancer? My original tumor had been estrogen-receptor positive, meaning it was dependent on estrogen for growth. Could the problem in my arm be hormonally stimulated? I had stopped taking tamoxifen two years after my mastectomy. That was a year ago.

I saw my oncologist and explained my theory to him. He insisted that I had tendonitis in my arm and told me to take some painkillers. He said he knew I was concerned about a recurrence of breast cancer, but that not every pain I got was going to be related to breast cancer. So, I went home, took my pills, and tried to stop worrying so much.

The pills didn't work. One night I woke up in the middle of the night, crying from the intense pain that had developed in my arm. I knew I didn't have tendonitis. I went back to the oncologist again. He finally suggested that I get an X ray of my shoulder, arm, and neck, because maybe I had a pinched nerve. It showed a shadow, and the doctor suggested I follow it with a bone scan. Progress at last! The scan showed a problem in the humerus bone. A bone biopsy was performed, and I awoke from the anesthesia to find my arm bound to my body. The orthopedic surgeon called to tell me we'd have to wait for the pathology report to get a diagnosis. I went home with instructions not to move my arm and waited.

Two days later my oncologist called. He said I had metastatic breast cancer. Not only did I have a metastasis, but I had had it the entire three years since my mastectomy. The cells from the bone matched the cells from my original tumor. The cancer had spread, undetected, before I had my mastectomy. How could that be? My lymph nodes had been clean. There was no indication at the time of my surgery that the cancer had spread beyond the original tumor.

Terror set in. As a volunteer, I had been teaching other women about the risks of breast cancer. To do this, I had educated myself all too well about this disease. I knew that breast cancer could spread to the brain, bones, lungs, and liver. I knew what the statistics said about recurrence and long-term survival. I knew I was in big trouble.

Because my case was considered somewhat unusual (metastases in the humerus bone are not too common), my case was reviewed by the tumor board at the hospital. My bone scan had indicated a metastasis only in my arm. When breast cancer spreads to the bones it usually appears in many sites (I was told anywhere from five to a hundred is common). But I had just one! The tumor board recommended aggressive treatment, including six weeks of radiation therapy, several months of chemotherapy, and removal of my ovaries (to eliminate estrogen in my system). Within a few days, I had the surgery to remove my ovaries, and I started the first of my twenty-eight radiation treatments. Approximately two weeks later I began five months of chemotherapy.

MY WAKE-UP CALL

If ever there was a "wake-up call" for me, this was it. The doctors weren't talking about survival statistics this time. I was facing a very uncertain future. I clung to the belief that I would be among those who survive recurrence.

In October 1992, just a few months after completing my chemotherapy, I participated in Portland's first Race for the Cure. It was an incredible day, one of the best of my life. Being a survivor and feeling the support of the six thousand women who ran or walked that day was an experience I'll always cherish.

It has been nearly five years since I was first diagnosed and nearly two years since my recurrence. I've had checkups every three months since the end of my treatment and have had three bone scans during that time. There is no evidence of any metastases in my body. I'm healthy again!

My journey has taken me through some dangerous curves, but I'm on a great road now and am enjoying every mile.

Kaye Walz
Beaverton, Oregon

This past July I underwent a stem cell transplant at Vanderbuilt University in Nashville. I had several complications, one being fluid build-up in my lungs. This was very critical as I had no immune system. I was placed on a respirator for several days. I have no memory of that period. The doctors told my husband they did not think I would survive, but I proved them wrong! I did improve, drastically, almost overnight. The doctors and nurses call my recovery miraculous.

There were so many people praying for me and I feel so blessed to be here today. My latest CAT scan showed "much improvement." I live every day to the fullest and thank God for the miracle of life.

The negative aspect of this has been my insurance company's refusal to pay for any of the transplant procedure. My husband is faced with a $140,000 medical bill. We have an excellent attorney who feels I have a chance of winning, but it will probably go to court. Wish me luck.

Best regards
Nancy Martin
Charlottesville, Virginia

Five years ago this month I was diagnosed with breast cancer. At that moment I thought it was the darkest period of my life. My tumor was almost 2 centimeters, and the cancer had invaded my lymph nodes—nine out of twenty-one were positive. I had a modified radical mastectomy, followed by six months of chemotherapy.

Getting back into my routine as a second-grade teacher really helped me to keep from constantly fixating on this disease. My treatments were on Friday afternoon, so I missed very little time from school.

I cannot say that since my breast cancer I have begun any new undertaking or that I have gone a different path in life. My life is actually pretty much the same. Two of my children have moved out of the house while they finish college—it was very hard for me to let go, but life goes on. I've learned I can't use my cancer to persuade the people I love, or the world in general, to do what I want.

Sometimes I find myself thinking that life isn't fair and wonder what I did to bring on this disease. Other times I feel life should give me only good things from now on. But I know that circumstances and life situations don't always change just because you've had cancer. A person doesn't have to go out and try something new and different to prove to herself that she has found inner strength and courage!

Rather, facing each day with an anticipation for life and an acceptance of whatever comes can demonstrate the greatest amount of courage and strength.

Life is life! None of us knows how long we have been placed on this earth. I only know that I need to live my life to the fullest—cancer or not—and that I can do this by keeping my attitude positive.

Sincerely,
Elizabeth H.
Aurora, Colorado

I come from a family where there was a lot of cancer. My mother died from breast cancer when she was only fifty years old. My brother died from cancer at forty, my sister at forty-three. I have always taken care of myself—eating right, exercising every day, and going for regular mammograms. Still, I worried. And the closer I got to forty, the more I worried. Forty, fortunately, came and went. At forty-three, again, came the fear, and again I managed to push it away. Then, at forty-eight, it happened. Breast cancer. Finally.

I sometimes think about writing a book about all this. If I did, I probably would start by telling how a very close friend of mine died at thirty-eight because, when she found a lump in her breast, she was afraid to go to the doctor until it was too late. I would write, too, about the first person who talked to me about her breast cancer and how she reassured me, and about how you should not be afraid to talk to people about it.

I would also write about how, right before my surgery, I saw my mother standing before me, blowing kisses at me, and about my faith in God, and how He was with me, giving me all the strength I need.

> My list goes on and on . . .
> Lois B.
> Grantsville, Maryland

First: a bit of background information on me. My breast cancer was diagnosed in December 1989 (at age thirty-two) with no "family history" anywhere. This was followed by two surgeries, six months of adjuvant chemotherapy, and thirty-five radiation treatments. Today, I am almost four years out (with no signs of recurrence, thank God).

I learned very early after diagnosis that it's always the "fear of the unknown" that makes everything so frightening. Of course everyone must deal with these issues in their own way, but mine was to try to make "known" as much as I could. For me, personally, it was education and information. The more I knew, the easier it was for me to deal with it, *and* the easier to explain things to my family and loved ones. I read everything I could get my hands on and, more importantly, I asked my oncologist a million questions.

A lot of newly diagnosed people put their complete trust in their oncologists, but they're only human. They don't know everything. Sure, they know more about cancer and oncology than their patients do, but there are still a lot of unanswered questions. Because oncologists deal with these issues on a daily basis, they often assume you—the patient— know more than you do. That's why I felt it was crucial to ask questions about everything.

173

Mentioning "family" brings up another related item . . . my mother. I truly feel that this ordeal was harder on her than it was on me. As a parent, it's much harder to deal with your child's illness (no matter what the age of that child) than if it were happening to you yourself. However, because I explained everything to my mother on a very medical/information level, it made things less frightening for her.

My husband and I have only one son (age six). We want very much to have another child and to get on with our lives. We have discussed this at great length with both my oncologist and my OB/GYN. My oncologist did some extensive research at his medical library to find out what the current statistics are regarding this topic. But, because only 6 percent of breast cancer cases are in women under forty (or of child-bearing age), there is not a lot of current data in print.

His findings were ". . . that there was no significant difference in the recurrence rate in women that did or did not have subsequent pregnancies *nor* did it seem to affect the long-term survival rates." There was one study that even suggested ". . . that those women who went on to have more children had better survival rates than those who did not."

In years past, the oncologists were advising all breast cancer patients of child-bearing age *not* to become pregnant, as it was felt at the time that the increase in hormone levels caused by pregnancy could help stimulate or promote growth or recurrence of the disease.

Today, the medical community has different data, theories, and studies looking at this issue. But the frightening part is that there is no concrete proof that "yes, this will happen if you get pregnant" or "no, this will not happen if you get pregnant." No one will be able to give you a definitive answer . . . it's all speculation/theory.

My oncologist's main concern is not that a pregnancy would promote recurrence, but that it would become more of a "quality of life" type issue. For example, how would my husband be able to handle a six-year old *and* an infant if I were to get a recurrence and perhaps die?

Based on all the information we have gathered so far and the many discussions with our medical professionals, my husband and I feel that if a recurrence is meant to happen, it's going to happen—regardless of whether or not we have more children. There's nothing we can do to prevent or change that fact. If that *is* the case and I *am* meant to have a recurrence, the bright side is that my son will always have a brother or sister. I guess the bottom line is that I refuse to live life always wondering "what if . . . ?"

Sincerely,
Lori H.
Arvada, Colorado

I was only twenty-six when I found out my lump was cancer. I immediately thought of my little daughter and the other children my husband and I had hoped to have. Why me? I wondered. Why now? I wanted to scream, to break things, to destroy! My husband said, "Throw eggs!" He took them from the refrigerator and I started with the sink. And I just kept going. (We still have egg stains on our ceiling.)

I wanted control and I took it. I knew I couldn't control the fact that I had cancer, but I felt I could control my recovery from it. The way I look at it is, everyone has a certain number of major dilemmas in their lives. I was just getting mine over early! You see, it's not so much where the cancer *is* that matters, but getting it out of our bodies and going on with life. So, I had a mastectomy. Then I underwent chemo. I was more concerned with losing my hair than I was with losing my breast. I was amazed at the quantity of hair we have on our heads. About two thirds of mine fell out, but I never did wear the wig I'd had made.

Now almost five years have passed. We now have *four* children. They, more than anything, are why surviving was—and is—important. On Easter morning this year, after barely making it through an explosion of chocolate, I stretched out on the couch to relax. Promptly all four of my bunnies joined me! New toys, candy, a new video—and they all wanted me! This is what my life is about . . .

Take care,
Kim C.
Springboro, Ohio

I was thirty-five years old with a twenty-month-old daughter when I was first diagnosed with breast cancer in June of 1989. I had a lumpectomy and follow-up radiation. My prognosis was excellent, and I felt very fortunate.

I also naively believed that was the end of it.

In February 1992, now with a year-old baby boy, I began to suffer headaches and backaches. I was told that I had Stage IV metastatic breast cancer. I had a tumor behind my retina, several on my lower spine, several in my liver and in my bone marrow. After numerous consultations and many sleepless nights, I decided a bone marrow transplant was my best chance.

I underwent a double transplant at Rush-St. Luke's Presbyterian Medical Center in Chicago. The first one was in June. I had five days of chemotherapy at ten times the normal dose. I spent three weeks in the hospital's Bone Marrow Transplant Unit, then six weeks at home. I had to be careful of infection, so I had to stay out of crowds. I couldn't even change my son's diaper. But at least I was home. I felt really good and was walking a mile a day.

I returned for the second transplant in September. I was given a 20 percent chance for a cure and a 10 percent chance of not surviving the procedure. These are very disconcerting statistics, but I also knew that 90 percent of women in Stage IV do not live past five years with conventional chemotherapy. What I didn't know at the time was that they'd found spots on my femur and chest that hadn't been touched by the first chemotherapy. I think it was the second transplant that took care of those.

The transplant itself is not painful, but it's uncomfortable. You have a fever. You're nauseated. You throw up. And there's always the fear that you're going to catch something. In the hospital all you can do is walk the halls, so you get to know the other transplant patients. When I was in for my first transplant I met a young woman who went home and then came back with pneumonia. She was in intensive care and then she died. She had a three-year-old son.

So the fear is always there. It never leaves you.

The second time around wasn't as bad physically, but emotionally it was very hard because I knew it could well be the end of the line. In the beginning you have your treatment schedule charted, you know what to expect, and you hold on to that. But suddenly, at the end, you think: What if it doesn't work?

The positive things I experienced throughout this time are many—an inner strength and a strong will to fight. After going through this experience I feel I can take on anything life gives me! My husband, family, and friends were wonderful. My faith in God is stronger than ever. I believe He directed me the whole time.

179

I am not unique. There are many women I have met who have had bone marrow transplants and are doing well—some are three and four years post-transplant.

I want women to know that a diagnosis of breast cancer does not have to be a death sentence. I urge anyone who is faced with this situation to be informed and aggressive in the course of treatment. Do not leave all the decisions up to the medical field. And to those of you who are facing transplant, I want to say this: We're in this club we don't want to be in, and you think it's never going to end. But always remember there's hope. Take one day at a time and never give up.

I'm living proof that it works!

Sincerely,
Nancy Arnold
Plainfield, Illinois

The tiny lump in my right breast was noticeable to me months before I went to see my doctor, but like millions of women I told myself it was nothing. I have fibrous breasts anyway and have had lumps examined in the past. Each month as I did my self-exam, I would make certain that the little lump hadn't changed or grown, because I believed that it was normal if it just stayed small.

Suddenly it seemed like every magazine I picked up had an article about breast cancer, and the more I read, the more nervous I became. All this time my lump stayed the same, but I was touching it more and more. By June I had my husband feeling my lump to see if it had changed or grown. He, of course, suggested seeing a doctor. I tucked his suggestion in the back of my mind and continued to discuss my fears with my friends at work.

Eventually I had an exam, which led to an ultrasound, which also showed two other lumps deeper in my breast. No fluid could be drawn on needle aspirations, and so an appointment with a surgeon was set up. My husband and I learned from him more than we probably ever cared to about my treatment options if the lump turned out to be cancer, which it did.

Soon everyone close to us knew. Some took it well, some didn't. We accepted the cancer right from the start and decided to take each day as it came. Some days were not as easy as others, but we held together. The oncologist said I should feel very fortunate I had found it early, but not to downplay it; it still was cancer. He gave me a 90 percent cure rate with a mastectomy or lumpectomy and radiation to the breast.

I opted for lumpectomy and radiation. An axillary dissection done later showed no positive nodes. I cheered with joy and thanks. Recovery went quickly. Radiation was scheduled for afternoons, allowing me time to go to work, to my treatment, and then home. Each treatment was routine. Strip from the waist up, put on a gown, lie on the table, expose my breast (which had become easier by this time, since I was so used to it). The therapist set the machine to the black marks they had put on my chest and away we'd go.

I always called it "The Zap," although I never felt a thing during the sixty seconds of treatment. The only discomfort I had was some swelling and dryness, which caused itching to the whole area on and around the breast.

The therapist discovered on day one that Jann Ryder is a positive thinker and would be a survivor. I had stories to tell, concerns and many questions to have answered. These women earned their paychecks during my treatments! They, and my nurse, were my support system at the clinic during the six and a half weeks I was there. I will never be able to repay them.

I hope I can spread the news that breast cancer is on the rise and that we, as women, need to deal with it by awareness and by turning our fear into the power to face reality. Stay healthy and get regular exams. If you find a lump, big or small, hard or soft, check it out! Get second and third opinions if you need to, but do *something* other than live in fear.

I am completing this letter the morning of my last treatment. As I finish my last sentences and get to work, I have tears of joy in my eyes.

I am a survivor!

Sincerely,
Jann Ryder
Trempealeau, Wisconsin

Ellen S. lives in North Haven, Connecticut. Her cancer was discovered at her six-week post-partum checkup after the birth of her third baby. When she sent this she had just finished a course of high-dose chemotherapy and was about to enter the Bone Marrow Transplant Program at Dana Farber Cancer Institute in Boston. She is thirty-six.

> *"This is a copy of a very personal letter I sent to our many incredible, supportive, loving family and friends. It sums up my attitude and was written to them from the bottom of my heart."*

To our dear family and friends:

I have not written any thank-you notes since my battle with breast cancer began earlier this year in May. I have decided that I must use my computer to do it now, as we have had an amazingly generous outpouring of love and support during that time. So, forgive the "impersonal" approach of a typed letter, and please take the words as they are meant from my heart.

I have written this letter a hundred times in my mind. I have searched for the appropriate words to express my overwhelming gratitude for the unbelievable support we have received from all of you. Your words of encouragement, prayers, phone calls, Mass cards, books, religious pins, cards, food, flowers, hats, scarves, assistance with the kids, and

184

much more are what has helped us to get through this. The hugs, the inspiration, the smiles, and senses of humor (mine managed to stay intact . . .) have been an integral part of my healing process. For the rest of my life (and I'm planning on a long one) I will never forget what you have done to "carry" us through this very difficult period in our lives.

I have just received my last dose of chemotherapy and will be preparing to go to Dana Farber Cancer Institute in Boston on October 28th for approximately three weeks. I will be receiving a Bone Marrow Transplant. I view it as my insurance policy to prevent me from ever having to go through this again.

As I look back over the summer, much of it is a blur. So much happened so quickly, but we dealt with things day by day and have made it through. I could never have done it without my "inner circle"—Brian and our parents. They have seen the best and worst of this ordeal, and have really been the "wind beneath my wings."

From the beginning I realized that although I did not like what was handed to me, I was determined to handle it. We had too much good in our lives to let this destroy us.

We have our three beautiful children. When I look at their little faces it is all I need to get myself to do what is constantly being requested of me medically, physically, and emotionally. I am thankful I did not find out about my cancer while I was still pregnant with Laura. I enjoyed a great third pregnancy, an easy delivery, and six weeks of bliss with my adorable new baby. I have had Rachel as my young, yet incredibly understanding friend and constant "helper."

And, of course, there's our Eric, my lover boy one minute and the next minute we're arguing over every morsel of food on his plate—a situation that kept my mind off my bigger problems!

Vicky hung in there with us, making sure I kept eating enough food (we decided she is no longer Mexican, but half-Jewish and half-Italian). In addition, I have the best family, the best friends a person could ever hope for, and the best medical help available. With all of these great things in my life, I knew I had to think positively and replace fear with pleasant thoughts, fond memories, and hope for our future. I do have an inner peace and joy—cherishing the gifts of the present moment. You become so much more receptive to the gift of life itself in its simplest forms.

I close this letter with tears in my eyes. And I once again thank you from the bottom of my heart for everything that you have done to help me heal. Please know that I will always be there for you in your time of need.

With much love and more thanks than you will ever know.

Ellen

Ellen wrote the following letters to her children on the night before she went into the hospital.

To my dear sweet Rachel (six years old),

As I leave for my bone marrow transplant, I feel I must write a letter to each of you to tell you how much I love you.

There are no words to describe the beauty I see in you—not only physically, but also from within; you are so grown up. Sometimes I worry that you carry the weight of the world on your shoulders. Those beautiful eyes, your face's smile—brighten my day many times, in fact, each time I look at you.

I know the last few months have been hard. We don't get to do all the special things we normally do together. But this is the last step now. I must go so that I may live to be with you, Daddy, Eric, & Laura. I have no real goals in life except to be with all of you and just be a good mother and good friend.

I look forward to your every achievement. You are so bright, so eager to learn. I thank you for your intense understanding for a girl of only six years. Thank you for the hugs, the homemade cards, your patience, and constant cooperation. You are a great gift to our family.

I plan to be at your wedding and there to help you with your babies. This has been a bad week and will soon be behind us.

Should anything happen to me, please know I'll watch over you from Heaven. I'll be loving you all the days of your life. Help Daddy to find someone new to complete the family again. Make sure she'll be a good mommy. I know I can count on you to pick! But that's "Plan B." We'll be going with "Plan A," which is that I'll see you in three weeks. Oh, how I'll miss you, but I'll count *each day until I can see you and hug you. After that, I'll con-tinue to get better. Put this far behind us.*

> With all my love forever,
> Mom

P. S.. Please continue to be the great big sister that you are to Eric & Laura. They are so lucky to have you. XXOOOXXO

To my dear son Eric (four years old),

If you didn't keep me so busy, I might have written in your diary sooner!! I am writing you as I leave for Boston for my bone marrow transplant to finish up my cancer treatments.

Please know how much I love your beautiful little face, how you melt my heart with all your intense love of life. There is no child with more passion than you. Keep that passion as you grow. Channel it to your best ability. Don't let it get in your way, my dear.

Continue to love Rachel, Laura, & Daddy. Protect your sis-ters as you grow up. Make them your best friends. Keep on hug-ging, singing, smiling, & loving life.

Learn to have patience, so as not to make life too difficult on yourself. You are a brilliant boy, bursting with energy.

I will call you. Please sing "Zippity Doo Dah" to me for the strength I'll need each day.

Please know I love you more than words can say. I cannot wait for these weeks to pass by quickly.

> With all my love,
> Mommy

My dearest Laura (six months old),

I feel I must write to you before I leave for the hospital. Of course, it is everyone's intention that all will go well. I plan to get through with this dreaded disease and get back to being a mommy.

Then, we'll catch up on all the hugs & kisses that were robbed from me over the last five months. Certainly, you've given me a lot. You are so beautiful. In my heart I know God would not give me such a precious gift like you and then not let me live to nurture you & watch you grow up. I always wanted three children. You are my final fulfillment.

With all my love & affection,
Mommy

XXOO
See you in three weeks!

I had breast cancer at the age of thirty-one. It was five months before I went to the hospital. By then, the cancer had spread to three ribs. A week later I had a hysterectomy. That was forty-seven years ago. I will be seventy-nine years old soon.

I often wonder if records are kept of breast cancer survivors. I hope so.

E. A. Z.
Allentown, Pennsylvania

A year ago this month I was diagnosed with breast cancer. As an operating room nurse, I've carried many breast biopsy specimens to the waiting pathologist and always silently prayed the frozen section would be benign. Now, I was the patient—a breast cancer patient—and I entered the terrifying new world of oncology medicine. In this new world, estrogen receptors, tumor markers, CAT scans, blood counts, and other tests became the markers that determined what the course of my disease and my days would hold.

Since September I've undergone a modified radical mastectomy, insertion of an in-dwelling line for chemotherapy, the complication of a collapsed lung, the placement of a chest tube, four months of chemotherapy, and, in June, breast reconstruction.

Cancer has changed my life. It is the worst thing and the best thing that has ever happened to me. A nurse of twenty-nine years, I've always felt I had to be strong—to be in control. I realize now the stress of trying to be a perfectionist—the perfect nurse, wife, and mother—was killing me. I've done a lot of soul-searching and am making changes in my life.

I reached out to the nearest cancer center and joined a

Breast Cancer Support Group before I had my mastectomy. In my mind at first I thought of them—of us—as "Ladies of the Club." I love and admire these women so much. We are an ongoing mentor group. My admiration for the women who've gone before me has no bounds. The courage, the humor, the strength, and the determination to live each day with as much grace and courage as they can muster is a gift we accept and pass on with love to the newly diagnosed coming behind us.

Yoga, offered free at the center, and meditation have helped me widen my horizons to free myself of poisonous stress and to get in touch with both my mental and physical world. I've developed a new love and enjoyment of classical music. How I have lived to be fifty-two years old without appreciating the beauty of Chopin, Bach, Mozart, I'll never understand. It lifts the spirit and satisfies the soul's yearning.

I've reached out to my family and been given all the loving support I could ask for. My husband cried with me. We grieved. And then we began to live and laugh at every silly thing that came up. My family lives all over the country, but we've drawn so much closer, as I struggled through my first months with cancer. They sent me dozens of cards, CARE packages, books, cartoons, and poetry. Every morning, even through chemotherapy, I forced myself to put on my makeup and then write to my family members and friends. Every day the postman brought the prayers and loving support from my family I so desperately needed.

We call each other weekly now and always complete our calls with, "I love you." In my previously undemonstrative family that would have been unheard of.

I've let go of a lot of repressed anger and resentments I didn't know I carried as excess baggage. I'm learning to love myself more, and thus I'm reaching out with love to others. The random acts of kindness from strangers have been heartwarming.

I've kicked my previous escapist addiction to romance novels. I wasted so much of my life, reading meaningless drivel. Now I can't find time for all the good books I intend to read. Several books were superb. They include: *Minding the Body, Mending the Mind* by Joan Boiysenko; *The Healing Power of Humor* by Allen Klein; and, of course, *Anatomy of an Illness* by Norman Cousins.

I walk the dogs with my husband each afternoon in the park—not for the exercise we're supposed to make time for, but for the sheer joy of being outside, enjoying nature. I watch the clouds, the trees in all their infinite arrangements, the birds, the ducks and rabbits, and so on. I feel the breeze on my cheeks and really enjoy the moment.

When death seems closer life becomes infinitely sweeter. I feel as strong mentally and physically as I've ever felt in my life. God has been good to me.

Sincerely,
T. J. England
Huntington Beach, California

This letter, also by T.J. England, was written as a follow-up, ex-actly one year after the preceding one

October 1994

It's two years this month since I was diagnosed with breast cancer. In these last two years I've changed a lot. At fifty-three years of age, I finally feel I'm a "grown-up." Cancer certainly helps you mature and put away the juvenile cop-ing mechanisms of your past.

The last year has been an especially happy one for me. In March I started taking Tai Chi classes and am so pleased with the effects of these exercises. They are both soothing and energizing, and I highly recommend them.

I still attend my Breast Cancer Support Group and have made some very dear friends that I will love all my life. We all know that life is tenuous. Several in our group have had metastases. We're learning how to deal with each other's pain on a deeper level. And, Lord knows, we laugh hard be-tween the pains.

Last week I felt a couple of new lumps in my axilla. After hearing a couple of my friends were facing a new battle with cancer I feared the worst. But my oncologist and sur-geon checked me out, and I'm all right at this time.

Only rarely now do I experience the fearful "what ifs?" "What if I don't live to wear that second pair of walking shoes in my closet?" "What if, a year from now, I'm not well enough to attend this Military Reunion which I've already paid for?" That sort of thing. Life is now weeks and months of optimism, interrupted by a couple of hours of "what ifs," which we beat back into the darkness.

With love,
T.J.

Nancy Rollman lives in San Luis Obispo, California. This letter to her friends was written midway through her chemotherapy. She's thirty-nine.

*H*i!

It was good to hear from you. My world has pretty much been turned upside down. . . . It's sort of funny to think of having a conversation and having you say, "How are you?" and my responding, "Well, I'm fine, other than the fact that I'm separated from my husband and have breast cancer!" I'd say I have a few challenges to handle this year.

Actually, the one that sounds the scariest but has the better prognosis for recovery is the breast cancer.

Last August I went to my OB-GYN to check out a lump that I had felt in my right breast. She basically blew it off and said it didn't appear to be a "bad" lump, but sent me to get a mammogram. The mammogram showed nothing and the report basically said "Come back when you're forty." So I was greatly relieved and went about my life. Then this past March I noticed the lump felt bigger. So back I go to my doctor, who still said she didn't think it was a bad lump, but this time she sent me to a surgeon for a second opinion. The surgeon did a needle aspiration, and the pathology report came back saying the cells were "atypical, highly suspicious for malignancy." That news was so shocking that I denied it at first, then went to talk to an acupuncturist (who said I had to find out if it was cancerous because she would not be able to help with cancer); checked and rechecked the reputations of the surgeon and pathologist; and checked out every book from the library on breast cancer written since 1990.

My surgeon ended up being a great doctor, but she had the bedside manner of a gorilla and was not a good communicator. At my second meeting with her, she threw around the word "mastectomy" so many times, it was like someone asking what kind of bread you want on your sandwich. She left me with the impression that she would be more than happy to cut off my breast! It finally took a meeting with a reputable plastic surgeon who spoke very highly of her work and who said he would send family members to her, to allow me to trust her with my body.

The next step was to do a biopsy, to see if in fact the lump was cancerous (80 percent of lumps are not). In my case the biopsy was actually a lumpectomy, because the plan was to remove the entire lump, since it was small and had changed in size. So, on May 20th, I had outpatient surgery and knew before I came home that the lump was cancerous (at this point my mother was still saying, "Maybe they made a mistake.") That was a Friday and by Saturday I felt absolutely normal, had no pain, just had this heavy, castlike bandage on my breast and was wondering what the scar looked like. I was back to work on Monday, feeling numb because of the results, but glad to go to work to keep my sanity. Later that week I had the bandages removed and was really pleased with the scar.

Since the lump was cancerous (for a while that's how I was describing it; I still couldn't say, "Since I have breast cancer . . .") the next step was more surgery to remove lymph nodes to see if cancer cells had left the site and were potentially traveling through my body. Cancer cells from the breast will only go to certain other places versus going anywhere; they go to the lungs, liver, and bones. This procedure was going to determine if I would be looking at chemotherapy as part of my treatment (versus just radiation therapy). Well, BINGO! Two of ten lymph nodes removed were also cancerous. That was a tougher surgery to bounce back from. The cut is made right at the base of your armpit, so it really takes lots of stretching to get the full range of motion back in your arm and you're stiff for weeks. Also, a particular nerve has to be cut and the feeling in your underarm is completely gone—forever—no more tickling under that arm! You also had this drain sticking out of your side for ten days—that was fun.

After all the diagnoses were given and treatments prescribed we went to the UCLA Medical Center for a second opinion. That was such a worthwhile exercise; the doctors there confirmed everything that I was told here, with a few minor differences of opinion (they're more conservative there), and basically said that my illness was so basic and caught early enough that with standard treatment I have an excellent chance of being cured and never having a recurrence.

So, on July 7th I started chemotherapy. It's administered intravenously at the doctor's office twice a month and takes about three hours each time. You get a combination of three drugs plus anti-nausea medicine. I was scared to death of all the side effects I kept reading about and came home expecting to sort of "explode" with stuff. Well, nothing happened—I even vacuumed the entire house that day! It was the first day of my time off from work (I'm on family leave, probably until I'm finished with all this), and I wanted the house to be in order for my new lifestyle. All in all, the side effects have been very manageable—one or two real low-energy days within the first few days after treatment, then pretty much back to normal, a few things here and there. I've had six treatments so far; six more to go, for a total period of six months. I'm not on the real aggressive drugs so I may not lose my hair, which is my most dreaded side effect of all. To be prepared, I got a wig. So far, I've had some thinning, but I still have HAIR!

Radiation started six weeks ago—that requires being radiated (just the right breast) every day for six and a half weeks. In comparison to the chemo, radiation is a breeze. Only a few more days to go.

The other side effect from both these treatments is potential cumulative fatigue because both of them are destroying cells, which then requires extra energy for your body to rebuild. But so far I am still going to the gym, taking vitamins, and eating super healthy, which I think is helping a lot. I decided I just didn't need the stress of working, with all the medical appointments, follow-ups, etc.. You have to go in weekly to get checked for low blood counts, and sometimes more often to get rechecked or get shots to boost your count. Last week, between radiation, a chemo treatment, and follow-up shots, I was at a doctor's office every single day including Saturday and Sunday.

The most shocking and upsetting side effect of chemotherapy is that it may chemically induce menopause—honest to God, that was a real kicker for me! My period will probably stop, I could get hot flashes, night sweats, mood swings—the whole enchilada. And, because of my age there will be more than a 50 percent chance of the menopause being permanent after I finish my treatment. Although I obviously have not been anxious to have children, I wanted the ultimate decision to be mine and I certainly didn't want hot flashes, etc., any sooner than necessary! So, at this point, it's still wait and see, because I have had my periods for these first two months, and I've had no other signs of menopause yet. The other detail here is that giving a woman estrogen after breast cancer is very controversial in the medical community because estrogen is all tied up to this breast cancer stuff (i.e., potential hormone imbalance since I've never had children, which puts you at greatest risk), so good luck getting hormone therapy, like estrogen, to help with menopause. I never thought I'd ever need to know about any of this stuff!

I'm absolutely loving not working. It's the first time in my adult life (about twenty years), that I have not worked, and it's sad that this is what it took to get me to take some time off. Gus, Sam, and Amber (my dogs) love having an at-home mom! And my dry cleaning bills have really gone down! Sam's hair is starting to thin, just because he's almost ten—but we're asking him if he's having sympathy pains for me! I've worked on small house projects, like finishing paint trim here and there, and other maintenance stuff; refinished some antique sewing spools. Next is to figure out a way to display my collection of antique ice cream scoops. A friend gave me a watercolor lesson book and some paints, so I am playing with those as a way to lighten up and get some other interests going, besides just working at work and work-ing at my master's degree.

Overall, this has been an incredible experience, and its only halfway through. The books I read in the beginning were so positive and upbeat that I've really had the attitude all along that this is an illness, is very treatable and curable and I'm going to take time for myself to deal with it and then get on with my life. It can happen to anyone who has breasts, and I just wish someone would discover its cause and its prevention. Curing it after you get it is way too late. What really saved my breast (i.e., a lumpectomy versus a mastectomy) was finding the lump early while it was still small. I've met several women whose lumps were too big to save their breasts. What I've found out about mammograms is that they have a 15 percent error rate, and it's a lot harder to x-ray lumps in younger women because our breast tissue is so much denser than someone's who is sixty (if I had known either of those two things, I never would have let my former doctor brush off my lump in the beginning of this process). The irony is that cancer in younger people is much more aggressive than in older people, so here we have modern technology that can't pick up cancerous lumps in an age group that really needs accuracy. In hindsight, that's why doctors are pushing us to do self-exams, so we can find lumps that perhaps a mammogram can't.

In terms of my marriage, I guess I'll start to wrap this up by saying that Greg's been living in the apartment above the barn since January. He's been supportive and helpful during this breast cancer stuff, but we certainly don't seem to be able to resolve our other problems, which are age-old and which I don't need to bore you with. I certainly am going to be a changed person after this experience, and I realize that I need to make some major changes in my life, so I don't know yet what will happen to the marriage.

Well, this pretty much brings you up-to-date with me. I hope you are fine and that your summer was a good one.

Love,
Nancy

I received this letter the morning that I was to deliver this book to my editor. It is from Jean Maynard, whose original letter appears on page 40. It seemed to me a perfect way to close this book.

*D*ear Ina,

I was recently in your neck of the woods. The purpose of my trip to Boston was business, the result of accepting a new job—I'm in sales of medical equipment now—I changed jobs around the beginning of the year. Interesting how things happen. I had spent thirteen years as a medical technologist at the hospital, as you know, and had not been actively seeking a new position. But this one just came along and after re-evaluating my priorities post-mastectomy, I decided I was due for a change. The truth is, although having had breast cancer still greatly affects my life, I don't think of it every day anymore.

I'm able to see sunrises regularly, now, something I couldn't do when I worked afternoon shifts at the hospital. It's given me a greater spirituality than before. It's a quiet spirituality, but it seems to pervade my whole being most of the time instead of occasionally. When I'm on the road I find myself singing "Amazing Grace" at the top of my lungs in the morning as I drive down the highway toward my destination for the day. What a show for the rest of the road warriors!

My ESP seems much more highly developed, and I seem to be intuitively doing the right thing. I find I cut to the chase a lot more easily. My prayers are oriented toward others than myself. There is a part of the Mass where the prayer is, "Let the Lord be in my mind, on my lips, and in my heart." I somehow modified it to direct my interactions with people on my job. As I drive toward the sunrise each day, I pray, "Let the Lord be in my mind that I may find the solutions to my customer's problems, on my lips that I may speak only the truth in my heart so that I can truly understand their needs." Lest you think that I went around the bend altogether, on occasion I still will have a few more beers than is probably good for me, use the "F word" on a more regular basis than is probably required, and admit to sneaking a cigarette every once in a while during social situations. That little bit of defiance is necessary to keep me who I am and keep things in perspective.

Jessie is a senior this year and doing very well. These training trips have enabled me to bribe him with hockey paraphernalia from the homes of the Boston Bruins, San Jose Sharks, Chicago Blackhawks, etc., so we seem to be experiencing a good place in our relationship. Mike is still on midnights but actively scrutinizing other positions as they arise. I think he feels a certain air of change as well. He has been wonderfully supportive of me in my new endeavors. I have no idea how I stumbled into his life but thank God that I did.

I'm so glad all our letters will be making their way into the world. It's apparently a very long pregnancy with books and publications, and hopefully you are able to eat in the meantime! I have really appreciated your keeping in touch and am looking forward to hearing from you whenever you find time. I hope you and your family are happy and well. Don't work too hard, and please take time to take care of and be good to yourself.

Love,
Jean

INDEX

207